RUSTY
ZIPPERS

In their earlier grades they had always joined each other on the playground swings but after Albert Ray convinced Al that if they moved the playground swing fast enough and high enough eventually the swing would make a loop and they would be the first in school to make a loop on the school swings. So each day they would make the swings go as fast and as high as they could. When the day came that Al went too high and the swing stalled and fell straight down; he held on for dear life as the fall from 15 feet high that broke the swing seat and one of the chains holding the seat. The teachers got involved and questioned their sanity and mentioned something called Physics that neither Al nor Albert Ray understood or believed because to them looping a swing was as simple as tying a rock on a string, holding the string in your hand and then swinging the rock until it looped around your finger.

RUSTY ZIPPERS

ALAN NEIL

RUSTY ZIPPERS

iUniverse books may be ordered through booksellers or by contacting:

iUniverse
1663 Liberty Drive
Bloomington, IN 47403
www.iuniverse.com
1-800-Authors (1-800-288-4677)

ISBN: 978-1-5320-8197-2 (sc)
ISBN: 978-1-5320-8196-5 (e)

Library of Congress Control Number: 2019913306

Print information available on the last page.

iUniverse rev. date: 12/18/2019

CONTENTS

GREEN RAILROAD

A fter America had finished its civil war and slavery plus the rights of individual states become less of a social issue; America started expanding. Railroads were built that allowed connecting the East coast to the west coast and all parts in between. Much of the Middle America was considered Native American Indian territories and the next American war was with the Indians. The impetus of trade between the gold and silver mines in the West and the goods and services from the East became a priority. The railroads became the way America traveled. Cattle drives from Texas to the rail roads in Kansas stopped in favor of using railroads to get cows to the markets in Kansas and Chicago. Wild West towns and cowboys were dying but the rails offered transportation to the lumber and grain industries from the heart of America and the only wars being fought were with the Native Indians. America was growing and expanding and making more money was everyone's concern. Side railroad lines also provided easy transportation between cities and small towns. For a relatively short period of time Americans traveled by rail. The baseball Hall of Fame is the perfect example of Americans traveling by rail. Today Cooperstown New York is considered in the middle of nowhere but when the hall of fame started any one could travel from every city that had a baseball team to Cooperstown. Old money investors from the East coast invested heavy into railroad companies and railroad investments produced some of the richest people in America. Dallas and Fort Worth became rail centers and the lines that reached deep in the heart of East Texas.

World War 1, the great depression and World War 2 quickly gave America a test. The biggest test was to see if America could shed its policy of isolation from its European roots and maintain its status and its freedoms. During these years the economy of America went up and down like a yoyo and the great depression made America stronger and forced people to a self-supporting status that would give most Americans pride than would push them to total victory in World War 2. America would label this generation as the Greatest Generation ever. The greatest generation of Americans was born in WW 1, grew up during the great depression and fought to total victory in World War 2. After the war was over manufacturing that supported WWII quickly converted to production for trade and improved living. Times were good but the parents of the greatest generation remembered great times followed by horrible times and also the horrible losses in the war. The war brought America into the atomic age. It was a frightening time for both war babies and baby boomers. Drills in all public schools were held to teach children how to survive atomic attacks but most families could afford automobiles and this gave them the liberty to just drive away. The generations of Americans would prosper for 3 generations and America's financial success would be a beacon in the night for the entire 3rd world. The beauty and strength of America had always been in its diversity of people, freedoms to speak and worship as they pleased. The great melting pot represented people from all over the Earth. No place on Earth offered freedoms like America guaranteed. Americans were a blessed people but the trails from Europe, Asia and Africa told long and sad stories about why these freedoms were so important. It also told sad stories about Native Americans being destroyed by invaders.

When Al discovered computers, made a living working with computers and the Age of Information came that enable searches of information on anything; he started tracking down his family history and how they got to America and the history of Native Americans who were already here.

It was common to know 2 or 3 generations of family history from what Parents and Grand Parents told grandchildren but with America expanding, family history was often miles away. Al's interest was tweaked by the fact that his aunts and uncles seeming to always knowing exactly what he was thinking. He started his research and there were not yet affordable DNA test to tell him about himself and his family. The knowledge came from court houses records, national archives and some very old newspapers. It became a hobby but it also enabled him to learn about his family. While growing up he knew so little about them. He never considered himself a simple person and he liked to choose his own path and develop his own interest.

Sometimes he seemed pressured to "just fit in" and he always went out of his way to not be a blind follower of someone else's ideas.

He quickly traced his father's family coming to America in the 1640's. The most unusual thing that he learned was most of their first names was repeated for 5 or 6 generations. Second important thing he learned was his grandmother was a Native American Indian. It helped him understand the family's love of nature; it helped him to understand their visions or as they said "flash forwards. It helped him to understand his great respect for all of God's creations. It helped him to understand their warrior spirits and the spirits of their ancestors but most of all he learned why ever single male member had served in the Army and earned their unspoken love of freedom. It helped him understand men who weren't warriors. I helped him understand because somehow those beliefs were totally ingrained in his soul without anyone teaching him or telling him.

His father's family came to America from Scotland in the mid 1600's and his grandmother's family was already there. His father's family came to the Carolinas and kept moving West until the trees stopped and the plains started. His Native Grandmother's family had lived in the East Texas forest as long as anyone remembered. Her people was a local band that was somewhat aligned with the Caddo Indians but when Texas became a state in America most Indians were relocated to Oklahoma, The remaining tribe members married within the new Anglo settlers. Al felt pride and a sense of belonging when he studied his father's family roots.

His mother's side of the family wasn't so easy to digest and understand. Most of his father's family was employed as working ranchers or bankers with an understanding that you should never work for the government (any government) and never sell family land. The men all served in the military during war. Most of his mother's family worked for the government and always sold family land as they migrated. They never viewed land as being special and very few of them served in the military.

Al's mother's family on her father's side came from a long line of religious Stallworth's. They also came to America in the 1640's. They originally came from France during the Protestant movement but had to move to England because of their religious beliefs.

They also had religious problems in England and came to America more than one hundred years before the American Revolution. They were some of the first settlers in America and prospered in the Carolinas with hard work, lumber making sawmills and farming. They were big, strong minded and physically strong hardworking people. When the first born son in America married a Cherokee Indian in the Carolinas they were criticized by their neighbors and the entire family moved to Northern Alabama. They obtained 640 acres of land and continued working with lumber sawmills and farming. They didn't move to Texas until the 1870's. The trip to Texas was without any stops. His mother's family was not warriors but they were big physical people who always defended their honor. It was only during America's civil war they were soldiers. Once they were locked in battle and they ran out of bullets. One of them stood up and challenged the enemy to a physical fight. They provided labor and materials to build the greatest church in Alabama but Church records show that most of the men were kicked out of the church for drinking, cussing and fighting. The trip to Texas was because they didn't like being occupied and suppressed by a conquering army and they killed some of the occupying forces. If they had been arrested and gone to trial death by hanging was a guaranteed outcome. No man's land in Texas became their home for a hundred years until eventually most of them moved to Houston. Houston seemed to be a perfect fit for their style of living. Grandpa had seven brothers and five sisters. Five of the brothers were working preachers. Three of the sisters were married to preachers. The brothers and sisters who were not preachers were drinkers and seemed to drink enough alcohol for the rest of the family. The drinkers all had successful businesses but the preachers families all preferred to work for some branch of the government. Al grew up with a complex understanding of serving his country in the military and he also had an understanding that he was a creation of God unlike any other creation but a part of all of Gods creations.

His mother's side of the family had some missing links. All of his grandmother's family was a mystery. Their roots started in an orphanage just south of Dallas. The orphanage was in Corsicana located 50 miles South of Dallas. Corsicana was home to the first major oil discovery in Texas and became a major railroad town. The railroads stayed busy moving the 800,000 barrels of oil per day to markets but also as a center for all the railroad connections to smaller towns. It was also the richest town in Texas for a few decades. Accumulating wealth was achievable for hard working and lucky people who lived there. During the late 1800's railroads were the blood veins that connected all parts of East Texas. The seven brothers and sisters grew up in the orphanage in the richest town in Texas. None of them were adopted by step parents and when the oldest became of legal age and released from the orphanage they started their adult life and after them getting married they each adopted the next oldest child from the orphanage. Each child adopted the next oldest child remaining in the orphanage and they continued this until the last child was adopted. They all talked about being put in the orphanage after their father died. They all claimed to be Comanche Indians like their father but they all had red or blond hair and very light skin. One thing that could never be questioned was their love for their brothers and sisters. They always showed unquestioned love for each other and their families. Their quick tempers and willingness to fight never applied to a family member. Their early lives were devoted to becoming successful and responsible enough to adopt the next brother or sister from the orphanage. Few of them felt compelled to serve in the military, be at peace with nature or saving the souls of strangers. The only noticeable personality trait was the all had artistic abilities. They could fashion beautiful objects without too much thought or plan. Art forms seemed natural to them and they never felt special because of their art abilities but they all were artist. The one thing missing from all of them was their sense of humor; they had no time for joking or laughing. It seemed so odd that children were raised by a Comanche Indian father because they all had blue or green eyes; red or blond hair and never spoke of their mother or real father. The orphanage had recorded their family name as Green but they never talked about their real father or mother. Al really doubted the Comanche Indian who raised them until he died, was named Green. Al never doubted that it was his grandmother who taught him how to believe in himself and how to dream but he never thought it was because he was her only grandchild who had Green eyes like his grandmother. His grandmother designed and made clothes for the actors in the main theater in Houston, her talents and creativity were apparent. During Al's early years his grandmother would design and sew the costumes for the Houston Theater and tell Al about the characters wearing them. Every character was a history lesson. The clothes she designed were from her brain and the pictures planted in her brain came from places she had never been to but she taught a 5 year old Al about life in New York, Paris and London. Al would later spend much of his life in those cities and always thought about how his grandmother knew so much about them in spite of the fact that during her life she never once traveled outside the State of Texas. When it was her turn to be adopted her older brother adopted her from the orphanage and he ran a successful leather business of making saddles and leather harness as the railroads were replaced by roads and horses. He was self-taught and his saddles were collector items of art that sold for top dollar. Years later the town would place a life size Bronze statue of him on the street outside his old store.

When Al's grandmother married his grandfather she entered into the world of a family with religion being the main focus of life. Saving souls and preaching the gospel was something she tolerated but her joy in life was working for the theater making costumes. It seemed that her creations had souls of their own. After grandma got married it was her duty to go to the orphanage and adopt her younger sister. Her younger sister was the last family member to be adopted and the oath they all made to each other was completed. Her younger sister married a government worker from Dallas and promptly had two sons. Her life was happy until her husband got murdered and she married "Uncle Lonnie" the Jewish gangster. Uncle Lonnie was somehow involved in her husband's murder but it was never clear what his involvement was. It was Uncle Lonnie who taught Al and his brothers about saving their own souls. Uncle Lonnie was accepted into the family and the men admired him because he had suffered thru Polio as a child and was unable to do physical work. He never hid his gangster connections from the family and explained his connections as "Just making a living." Al would always remember him for his hats and Buick cars but Al and his brothers were taught by Uncle Lonnie to not do things just because they could. A trip to the Texas state fair had caused them problems. When Al and his older brother Joe were 14 and 16 years they went on a school trip with the Future Farmers of America. The trip was for 3 days and they stayed in a hotel in down town Dallas. Around the block from the hotel was a strip tease club. Laws were such that the teen agers could visit and watch the strip tease acts but they could not drink alcohol. The boys watched and before departing Joe received an 8 by 10 photo of one of the strippers. She autographed it by signing her name and saying "Good Luck Joe." When their mother found the picture hid under his bed she went crazy and demanded that their father punish them. When questioned they explained the current laws of Texas in Dallas. Things cooled down for the boys until the visit by Aunt Carrie and Uncle Lonnie. Mother told the story about the photo and while Aunt Carrie thought it funny, Uncle Lonnie was concerned. Later out of the presence of others Uncle Lonnie told them very clearly "They must never go to that place again". He explained in certain terms that "he knew the owner and he was no good, he is the kind of person who gave businessmen a very bad name. Ever since he came down from Chicago he has been nothing but trouble, we will take care of him when we can." The owners name was Jack Ruby. A few years later everyone knew exactly who Jack Ruby was. Thanks to Uncle Lonnie the boys knew who he was before they did.

It was apparent how much Uncle Lonnie loved Aunt Carrie and how much he and Aunt Carrie loved Al's family. Each year Aunt Carrie and Uncle Lonnie would drive from Dallas so Aunt Carrie could make new school clothes for Al and his brothers. She made the pants and shirts from scratch with the new materials like nylon and cotton synthetic blends she had purchased in Dallas and even though Al and his brothers rarely wore anything except short pants during summer months they were the best dressed kids in school wearing clothes made by Aunt Carrie. During their visits she gave updates on all family members and their successes. She loved to share their successes. She would also bring leather belts and wallets made for the boys by their Great Uncle. Each belt and wallet had their names tooled on them.

The mystery with his mother's mother side of the family was never clear until it was perfectly clear.

Computers Al told about the richest woman in New York City. Her family had made and lost a fortune from their Whale oil business. The story told how she made her own fortune by being the smartest investor on Wall Street during the great depression and how prudent she was with her money and how hard she worked to earn her fortune. She understood that all money must be invested to grow. She was forced to be a single mom after her husband died and left her almost in poverty. The computer told how she became the joke of Wall Street when her young son broke his leg and she tried to get him medical attention in a charity hospital but she was refused service because she had too much money. She chose to let her son grow up with a crooked leg because she would not spend investment money to get proper medical attention and after she became the joke of Wall Street because she was too cheap to pay for medical services for her son. It also told how she became the richest woman on Wall Street. All of this happened before women were allowed to vote in American elections. It told how she was taught by her Grandfather as a child how to do accounting and how good she was at accounting for money. Mostly it told how she beat the boys at their own game of building wealth. After she reached the pinnacle of success the jokes about her being too cheap to get her own son's broken leg fixed became intolerable so she sent him to Texas to oversee the rail roads that she owned. Her son enjoyed being out of New York and living on the railroads; He had his home in railroad cars and traveled freely as he watched the railroads die a slow and painful death. Roads were being built and automobiles were available and were replacing all the horses and wagons; the rails were being discontinued to small towns.. The son's life was spent riding the rails in his opulent life style that included being with his girlfriend and fathering children. It all went bad when the queen of Wall Street made a surprise trip to Texas to see the actual reasons why her railroads were losing money. She found her son living with his girlfriend and fathering children. She had to fix it because she knew that her son's illegal children were entitled to her fortune. She made a quick deal with the girlfriend and mother of her grandchildren. She gave her a few million dollars and a ticket to Florida where she would live the remainder of her life with the rich and famous. She sent her son back to New York to work for her and to make sure there would never be a legal connection to her precious money. She hired a Comanche Indian to care for the children. He was paid well and raised the children until he passed away and the children were rounded up and placed in the orphanage. She went back to New York, sold her properties in Texas and gave no thought to her grandchildren's welfare. Case was closed and by the time Al found out the truth all of his grandmothers brothers and sisters were dead except for Aunt Carrie. She as in her 80's and lived alone after Uncle Lonnie died. Al went to visit her to learn if she knew who her mother and father was. Not too much to Al's surprise she knew the entire story as did all her brothers and sisters. She told that the family of orphans knew and remembered their real mother and father but while in the orphanage they all promised that none of their own children would ever know the truth about how they became orphans. Aunt Carrie made Al promise to never tell what he had learned. When Al questioned her as to why it was important to her that no one in the family should know the truth she simply said "Do you think the children should know how uncaring and heartless their Parents and Grand Parents were? Do you think it would help them?" Al promised to never tell the true story to anyone and secretly he hoped that his Great and Great, Great Grandmothers DNA had been wiped out by his Native American DNA and the DNA from the rest of his family. He never once thought about his unusual childhood hobbies of making money by selling garden seeds, waking up at 2 AM to deliver the morning newspaper and using his hard earned money to buy savings bonds.

PRACHINKO

Speedy was living in Jakarta Indonesia and it was a daily challenge to just live there. The challenge was to mingle and mix in with 10 million legal residents and 3 million illegal residents. The town traffic was a mixture of rich people riding in Mercedes driven by poor people or poor people driving weather beaten 30 year old Toyota's. Each of the great traffic circles in Jakarta provided entertainment by watching the beat up Toyotas drive near a new Mercedes and forcing them to the inner circle and robbing them of any possible exit. Traffic also had a peculiar mix of delivery trucks and fully packed city busses. It seemed that everyone who lived there was always on the move and he normally traveled to and from work in a Taxi that was always stuck in traffic circles.

He worked at two jobs to fight boredom and stay out of trouble. He originally came to Jakarta to work for an oil company as a financial analysist and the job was not challenging because to him it was simply taking numbers and formatting them into reports that measured financial success or failure. Every company had too many employees and getting numbers was easy. Getting good numbers was more of a challenge and the company that hired him wanted a professional numbers guy. Speedy was good with numbers but he was not proud of it because numbers got people fired, numbers got entire companies bought and sold; Numbers changed people's lives and effected their children. Numbers didn't always measure success because numbers didn't always measure the harm done to people or the environment. Numbers sometimes fueled corruption and destroyed or misguided populations. Speedy was very good with numbers and the company knew it. He had no oil company complaints when he accepted a second job.

His second job was working for Indonesia's retired Minister of Finance. A man who had fought for the independence of Indonesia and he was a man who helped kick the Dutch Masters out of the country;

A man who loved all the people and every part of his country. Speedy had met him during a sales presentation and they became friends for life. He showed Speedy the beauty of Jakarta and of Indonesia' people. In the heart of the city was a well-hidden golf course. The Minister loved the game of golf as did the President of Indonesia who also played there. Speedy spent time playing golf with the Minister but he didn't have any passion for golf. It seemed the more he played the worse he got because he lacked concentration and his 250 yard drives always created havoc. Speedy was a baseball player and he approached golf as a baseball player. He did manage to provide humor to the Minister with his short game but he could never appreciate why a one foot putt counted the same on the score card as a 250 yard drive. The golf course was constantly being carefully hand manicured by dozens of grounds keepers. All were women dressed in their best fully clothed Batik and wearing rounded bamboo skin hats. The Minister showed Speedy how to have fun on the course by asking one of the large breasted grounds keepers to show them her boobies. After negations the amount of tip to be paid, she obliged. The Minister was in his 80's but he did this every time the game got boring. The minister also won every match but never boasted about his game. Speedy had started playing golf after he had read the great Ben Hogan's book but he never practiced what Ben wrote about. The Minister was fun to be around and Speedy accepted his job offer without reservations.

He first met the Minister during a sales presentation that was being made at a 5 star hotel in the heart of Jakarta. Speedy's friend from Texas had requested that he attend to give advice on the numbers. The friend of Speedy had lived in Jakarta for 5 years and he knew who made decisions about spending Indonesian money. Speedy had been working in Indonesia for 5 years but his time was spent working in the jungles of Sumatra.

He spent few non-working days in Indonesia because Singapore was just a quick airplane or boat ride away. Singapore was a great place to recover from working in the Sumatran jungles. Time spent in Singapore was well spent mingling with tourist, getting medical attention when required, and eating great food in open air cafes, seeing 1st run movies or the landmarks that told unusual stories of British Colonial times. Singapore was a modern city but it was a lazy town much like the lazy Louisiana swamps that slowly moved water into the Gulf of Mexico but always preserving and protecting the life of the swamp. Like the swamps, Singapore had creatures that could rise up and attack. Speedy liked Singapore as a place to relax.

His Texas friend had spent most of his working life living in Singapore. Speedy knew that Singapore was built by the resources of Indonesia and Malaysia. It was also a haven for Americans who had worked in Vietnam during the war as contractors and were unwilling or unable to go home. Mostly Singapore was home of pirates and a safe haven for Chinese and British colonials with no other place to live. Most were unable to live in other parts of South East Asia because China was closed for business. It was a good place for profiteers. His friend saw opportunities in Jakarta so he moved there but Indonesians didn't trust the Singapore people because of their attempt to take over Indonesia. The Indonesian Army had gone on a Chinese killing spree numbering millions of dead Chinese after the attempted government takeover during 1965 and the wounds of their new freedom as a country were slow to heal. The fact that during the 400 year Dutch rule of Indonesia they had brought most of the Chinese to Indonesia as ruthless tax collectors really didn't help anything.

He attended the sales presentation with caution because his friend's company was from Singapore but his sales product was made in Texas. It was a product produced as a bi product of the chemicals they made for profit and it was considered waste products from the chemicals they made in Texas. Texas provided no means for them to dispose of the waste in Texas so they targeted exports.

Before the meeting Speedy had contacted his friend who was a professor at Texas A&M University and he was told that it should not be used for building roads. He was told in precise detail how the product was toxic and how it would contaminate water tables under the road; he said it shouldn't be used for anything. The Singapore Company wanted to sell it as a sealant for building roads in Indonesia.

The meeting was ready to start but everyone waited more than an hour for the retired Minister of Finance to arrive. When he arrived he apologized for being late and he blamed it on Jakarta traffic. Then he said "We can build big and beautiful cities, we can manage our Military and our natural resources but we have to learn to make better people who know how to drive or we will never be successful." Speedy became enraged as he thought of all the lives in balance because of the recent Presidents mandate to repopulate the 17 thousand Islands of Indonesia with political misfits from Java. His program was called Transmigration. He remembered seeing the transmigration people struggle as they adapted to life in the jungle. He said nothing as the Minister continued. Then he said "Mr. Minister if you think your cities are too good for your people, I suggest that you go back to see the villages of your ancestors; talk to them and learn what their values are. I have worked with and lived with some of those people and I am impressed with their personal and family values." Everyone in the room was shocked and his Texas friend said "You just screwed up." The Minister left the room and some of the others also walked out.

Speedy was upset with himself until a few minutes later the minister returned, walked up to Speedy and said "I like you, please join me for dinner." The others left to go home while the Minister and Speedy went to diner and talked about his childhood living under

Dutch rule, he told speedy about not knowing what money was and him seeing his first money, and speedy told him about his childhood and collecting pennies. He told the Minister the dangers of the product that his friend was selling. They became friends for life, shared decisions and proposed financial deals in private. The Minister and Speedy became family and they treasured each moment together and the Minister introduced him to some his Texas friends. Speedy wasn't surprised that he had rich and powerful Texas friends.

The minister appreciated Speedy speaking Bahasa Indonesian because he knew it was difficult for him to learn another language but Speedy learned to speak Indonesian the hard way. First he learned words, then he learned sentences, then he learned structure and suddenly he learned to speak fluent Indonesian. He could talk to ever day people and he enjoyed talking to them. Most oil company employees could not speak fluent Indonesian but to Speedy speaking to them in their own language opened up a new world of thought. Some oil company people didn't like him speaking Indonesian because they encouraged Indonesians employees to learn English.

Once in Sumatra a village of people had attacked the oil company's pipeline crew with axes and machetes. Speedy was sent along with a government official to solve the problem. When Speedy talked to the Village Chief he asked him very direct "What do you want?" The Chief told Speedy he wanted the pipeline crew to show respect for the Village and its people. Speedy told the Chief the pipeliners were good people and with the Chief's blessing the pipeliners would pay for a party so the people from his village and the pipeliners could get to know each other. The chief told him he would host a get together party if the pipeliners would pay for it. Speedy agreed and the government agent paid the amount the chief requested for the party. The Australian pipeliner in charge told Speedy "I saw you give him money and I think that what you did was wrong." Speedy told him to report him to his boss and he did. Speedy's boss wanted to know what happened and why Speedy told him to just take it from his payday. Speedy told him the party cost about $100 and we are spending $1200 per hour for heavy equipment standing idle because of the lack of respect shown to the Village. His Boss told speedy that he would arrange and send food, beer and a band to play music to the village so everyone would have a good party. The village was a Christian Batak tribe and beer drinking allowed.

The boss then transferred the Aussie to a different work location. The Chief and Speedy became friends and would visit often when the chief had concerns. Once he came to ask that the above ground pipeline to not be insulated. Speedy told him the insulation was for protection of his people because the pipeline had hot oil inside and the oil heated the pipe and the people may get burned. The chief explained that the village used the hot pipeline to dry fish. After drying the fish they could sell it for 10 ten times the price of wood smoked fish because the pipeline was the right temperature to dry fish that lasted longer; allowing them to put it on a bus and transport it to the large cities for sale. Against company regulations and safety practices the pipeline never got insulated and the fish oil kept the pipeline rust proof. Warning signs were posted by the Chief. Getting more money for their fish helped the village. The trucks hauling the fish came to the village empty until the chief started using profit from the fish to buy and transport bricks for use in home building. Speedy always felt good when he saw the trucks of bricks coming into the village and the dried fish leaving going to markets.

In the meetings with the minister everyone was educated to speak English. Speedy knew he spoke Indonesian and English without regard to finesse. In one meeting the Singapore guest was talking to the Minister with strong terms. Speedy got upset and told them in Bahasa Indonesian that the meeting was over and for him to please leave. Later the Minister told Speedy to "Please never speak in Indonesian language again in a meeting with a foreigner because you are using street words spoken from your heart and they are painful to hear. You are speaking like a man on the street." With tears in his eyes Speedy told him "I am a man on the street." The Minister laughed and hugged him like he was his father. After the meeting the Minister told Speedy "Do you want to go out and find some young women. An American whispered to Speedy "Is he a pervert?" Speedy laughed because he knew the Minister was all business and he told the American "Be very careful because he is 85 years old and when he says young women it means someone in their 70's."

The meetings to provide financing for development projects required a lot of preparation. Government officials must be advised and risk must be identified. Normally the Minister was in a good mood but one night he told Speedy that he really didn't understand people because he had requested a meeting with a young man he had hired and trained when he was the Minister of finance. The man wanted to be paid for meeting with him. The Minister told Speedy I will send him documents to review but I will send to him via a beautiful young lady who works for me. I will arrange the meeting at a hotel where I have rented a room and I will tell her to be all business and get the papers signed. The Minister laughed as he told Speedy of his plans. Speedy told him that he had never used a beautiful young lady to bring information to him and he was hurt that he only sent his driver.

A week later at Speedy's apartment the doorbell rang and Speedy looked thru the peep hole and saw no one. A few moments later the doorbell rang again and Speedy looked thru the peephole he saw a woman's stomach and belly button. He opened the door and a beautiful woman was holding a package of documents which she said the Minister wants you to review and sign. Speedy looked up in the 6'5" woman's eyes and saw a smile as she looked down on the 5"9" Speedy. He invited her in and then asked how she got her belly button all the way up to the front doors peep hole. She laughed and said "I used the chair that was next to the door." She told Speedy she had been a professional Basketball player and had played professionally in Australia and the Minister had told exactly what to do. The minister later called to make sure the message and documents were delivered and Speedy said yes everything was in order. Speedy made no mention of the woman then the Minister told Speedy "She is really tall and I thought you might enjoy seeing a beautiful woman who is tall. They laughed and Speedy told him "I do owe you one." Later deliveries were made by his driver.

Many projects were financed as results of their work and the money always came from a Bank in Switzerland that was owned by the Ministers billionaire friend in Texas. Speedy would later meet his billionaire friend and he would become a friend for life. A man Speedy loved and trusted a legend in Texas and a man who hated bad and loved all good things. A man who once was a member of the "Flying Tigers" who flew war goods over the Himalaya mountains to help defeat Japan in China during WWII. Speedy never once had an uninteresting or dull moment with either of them even they were both older than his father. The visits to Switzerland were all business but the respect of the bankers he received was because of his two friends. They appreciated that Speedy handled their money as if it was his own.

Speedy didn't like Switzerland because as he stood above the giant gold vaults containing most of the world's gold he could only think of the gold that came from peoples teeth after they were murdered in WWII. He could only think about Switzerland being a neutral state in Europe during a world war but his visions of money being used to make the world a better place to live made him smile and having two great friends who agreed with him made him happy.

One trip to the Swiss bank went bad. The Texan who owned the Swiss bank was busy, his bank's CEO was busy and the Minister was also busy. They had others doing their work. The Texan assigned his step son and the Minister assigned someone he trusted but lived in Singapore. Speedy was also busy with the oil company's new discovery in a remote part of

Indonesia. The discovery was made after all the previous exploration wells had come up showing no oil or gas. The discovery was purely accidental because the well was tested and showed no sign of hydrocarbons but the monsoon rains made it impossible to demobilize the drilling rig and the drilling contractor commanded a 75% standby rate be paid. Speedy's boss was very upset. He told Speedy "I ain't going to pay anyone to sit on their ass and complain about how bad the food we send via helicopter is." During the standby he made them retest and make new logs. He noticed the test results were different from the first and sent it to a consultant for reconciliation. The consultant decided the logs were inconclusive because they had encountered some magnetic or radioactive interference. The contractor was made to test each irregularity on the logs and to everyone's surprise the identifying oil and gas started by fingerprinting the oil and gas from each test level chosen by the boss. At the end of the day a discovery was made for 7 new and different oil and gas fields from one single oil well. Everyone at the oil company became very busy.

Speedy was requested to go to Zurich for 2 days to oversee the financial transaction. It was only 20 million dollars and should have gone without any problem but there were problems. Speedy looked at the documents/bank guarantees/project details but it was too late because they were already there and he was uncomfortable. He requested a private meeting with bank officials and told them in private that he suspected something was wrong. The bankers checked and found the bank guarantees to be forgeries. He immediately thanked the bankers and then he went crazy. He humiliated the Minister's associate and the Texan's step son. He traveled alone back to Jakarta. A few days later the Texan called him and told him that he did not appreciate him roughing up his son in Zurich and he wanted him to come visit him before he would have any more deals with the Minister. Three weeks later Speedy drove from Houston to Dallas to meet with him. He arrived exactly on time and waited 2 minutes before the Texan came out to meet him. He told Speedy that his meeting with the oil Minister from Qatar was running late and he told his secretary to take Speedy to his office to wait. Speedy was seated at his conference while he waited and he noticed the conference was made from Teak and rosewood. Embedded in the 5 meter long conference table was a collection of coins. They were Roman coins. He used the viewing glasses to look at them. Some were more than 2500 years old and all Speedy could think was it was possible that some of the coins had been used as payment to betray Jesus Christ, the Son of God...

The Texan came in and apologized for being late. He asks Speedy what happened in Zurich and Speedy explained exactly what had gone wrong and apologized for losing his temper in Zurich. As they sat next to each other at conference table the Texan started to cry and tell him about his Step son. He had raised him since was 2 years old, had educated him in Texas and in the best East coast business schools but he had a drug problem. He explained that he had the CEO of his Swiss bank be with him at all times so he couldn't drift into drugs while in Europe, he explained how much he loved him as he cried. Speedy looked away as the Texan cried and he noticed there was only two photographs framed and setting on his empty desk. One photo was of the Texan and the Flying Tigers Airplane he had flown in WWII and the other was a recent photo of him and the golfing great Ben Hogan. Speedy commented that he liked his photos and he stopped crying long enough to tell him Ben had Alzimers and he had placed him in a long term care facility nearby and he visited him each week. He had no family to look after him. He said they had grown up together. He said nothing about the Flying Tigers airplane picture, it spoke for itself as it showed what the Texan did and how a younger version of himself looked. When he spoke of Ben his tears stopped and he found strength to continue.

He then completely surprised Speedy by asking him if he was the son of Omer or Jesse. They were Speedy's father's brothers. Speedy told him that they were his Uncles and Archie was his father. He never explained how he knew Speedy's family. He invited Speedy to visit him and stay at his home whenever he could. On the drive back to Houston Speedy cried when he thought of his Uncles and father and his Texan friend.

A week later Speedy was back in Jakarta telling the Minister that all was well with the Texan and he was ready to work but he would no longer work with his Singapore friend. The Minister spoke as his face showed anger. It was the only time Speedy saw anger in his face but all he said was "Dam Prachinko." Speedy was both understanding of the minister and hurt because the word meant Chinese and the highlight of his time spent in Jakarta was helping Indonesia having a Prachinko as his lover and friend, someone that he would never forget.

Less than 5 years later the Minister passed away and a short time later the Texan passed away. The oil company's new oil and gas discovery produced such good numbers that they made the oil company a target for a buy out and it was sold to a larger company. Speedy left Jakarta after the oil company was sold and he would never again go to Jakarta, Dallas, or Switzerland.

His memories of his friends that he cried with would never go away.

The projects they made possible was books for schools in Java and Sumatra, growing bamboo forest for the artist in Bali, and creating doctors and hospitals for all. One of the projects that Speedy had concerns about was for a food company to add nutrients into the rice noodles. Noodles that all Indonesians ate when they had nothing else to help them survive. It was a project that required getting the Indonesian government to pass legislation defining the requirement to meet

ALAN NEIL

nutrient requirements in their product. 10 years later in a Houston supermarket he saw the same company's noodles for sale. He felt a little better about dealing with the government..

THE UNEXPLAINED

Funerals are the most likely the place to witness the unexplained. Sai and Freddie had been married for almost 40 years and her body started failing until finally it stopped. They were friends with Neil and Gale for 44 years. Freddie and Neil had spent a career working together, found each other multiple jobs, gone thru hard times together, and both were amazed at their friendships. Never once did they question their differences. The difference was great but not as great as their friendship. Freddie had grown up with two brothers in Northern California. He hid in College and feared being in the military. Neil had grown up with two brothers in East Texas, loved hiding in the National Forest and feared not being in the military. They met their wives at almost the same time. They had gotten married in a joint marriage ceremony in

Las Vegas. They returned to Las Vegas to celebrate their anniversary for 38 years. They had watched their children grow up and each other grow old. The four of them had little in common but they treasured their friendships and their children had become friends.

Their wives were just as different as they were even though they both came from Thailand. Sai came from East Thailand near the Cambodian border and Gale came from the South East part of Thailand. Both had been married before and each had a daughter. Sai's husband had fallen in love with a woman from Germany; He abandoned Sai and his daughter and moved to Germany with his new bride. Gale's husband had been in the army; got himself killed over a gambling problem and left Gale and his daughter to survive. Her family had not liked her husband and offered no help and she struggled at running an early morning restaurant for fishermen. Neil had met her while drinking coffee at 4 am trying to get sober enough to understand why Freddie could not bring a woman he had just met into his hotel room. Freddie was drunk and didn't understand why bribery didn't work after 3 am. .

Gale worked at odd jobs to support her daughter. Her X husband's mother adopted the daughter, her X husband's twin brother was a policeman in Bangkok and he helped raise her until she was 12 years old and moved to America with to live with Neil and Gale but through her life Gale paid all the bills. Sai was very forgiving and generous, Gale was very conservative. Years later Sai invited her X husband to stay with them when he and his German wife came to Los Angeles even though he never help Sai support their daughter. Neil was pretty sure that Gale's X husband would have been killed by Gale's family or himself if he had not already been killed. Sai and Gale had as many differences as Neil and Freddie. Freddie ancestry came from Denmark, Neil's kin blood lines were from Native American and Scotland. Sai's ancestry was mostly from the ancient Kramer of Cambodia who appeared Indian like and Gale's ancestors were from middle South China. Somehow they all seemed doomed to being lifetime friends. They laughed together, cried together and could call each other for help at any time.

Neil and Gale made a 2 day drive from Houston to Las Vegas to attend her funeral and so they could reflect on the last 44 years of being friends with Freddie and Sai. The long drive went thru Central and West Texas on to Santa Fe New Mexico and Arizona. Most of the trip was made in silence. No talking, no radio just thoughts of Freddie and Sai and a reflection of themselves.

Time had tested their strange friendship but never came close to breaking it. Over the years the relationship had been tested but never strained. Once while Neil was working in Indonesia and Freddie was working in Saudi Arabia they were able to spend a few days together. Sai had some family business to attend to and Freddie was left alone in Bangkok. He called Neil and told him that he was bored. Neil told him to go visit the waterfall just outside his hotel. Under the waterfall was an unmarked and unnamed massage parlor but the girls working there were airline stewardess who was doing flight layovers and staying in the same hotel as Freddie. Freddie visited the waterfall brought a girl back to his hotel and the two of them toured Bangkok. The girl left before Sai returned but she forgot her camera in Freddie's hotel room. After Sai came back the girl returned to get her camera and all hell broke loose. Somehow both Sai and Gale blamed Neil for telling Freddie about the place and Gale demanded to know exactly how Neil knew about the waterfall. He told her that he learned about it while he was getting a haircut. This was true but he didn't tell her that one of his friends had played a joke on him. He was on his way home from Papua New Guinee and he had a stopover in Bangkok. He never fooled around in Bangkok after he bought some Doves from a Buddhist Temple and set them free to carry away his sin of being an unfaithful husband. It worked and he was always on his best behavior in Bangkok. His friend from Kuwait was staying at the same hotel and wanted Neil to go with him exploring the Pat pong red light district but Neil said no. He explained that his goal for the day was to get his hair cut. His friend told him he knew just the place. The place looked like a real barber shop complete with antique chairs that lowered to a full 180 degrees. The waiting room had several good looking women dressed like barbers but after Neil chose one and got in the barber chair things changed, The woman put the barber chair in the 180 degree position, pulled down is pants and tried to sit down on top of him. He refused and told her to stop, he got out of the chair and

43

told his friend who was laughing to pay any expenses and walked out without his friend from Kuwait. He walked down the street and stopped in front of the 2 story waterfall for a cigarette, and then he went in the unmarked building under the waterfall. He thought that a real massage was in order; he had no idea about the wayward airline stewardess. In Freddie's story Neil was the bad guy for telling him about the waterfall and somehow Gail and Sai agreed with him.

Freddie had once gotten Neil a job working for the Los Angeles Department of Transportation. The job was boring a tunnel underground from West Hollywood to Hollywood and stopping at the underground station at Hollywood and Highlands. Neil's office was next to the Hollywood walk of fame. The previous contractor had been fired because their underground work had caused some of the Hollywood walk of fame to sink and destroy some of the old stars that lined the street. If there is anything holy in Hollywood it's the old actors star on the walk of fame. The job was difficult; the contractor was a well-connected, know it all California mafia company.

Hollywood changes faces when the tourists leave. Neil always arrived to work early and the real

Hollywood is just going to bed at sunrise. Freddie was having fun watching Neil view Hollywood in the early hours. The office was in the same building as the Hollywood High school classes for "the sexually confused students." Neil got to meet some of them during his smoke breaks and thought they were just kids finding their way but on a few occasions a Hollywood cop would show up during the smoke breaks and question them about something. Usually the subject was about a confused kid robbing a pervert. It all seemed pretty normal to Neil. When one morning Freddie called to check on him Neil was having breakfast at the McDonalds across the street. He had noticed the same homeless crowd each morning stealing food from anyone not looking and he had noticed a lot of men dressed like women and wearing pink or purple wigs. The crowd had also noticed his cowboy boots and clothing and no one seemed to care how the others were dressed. Freddie let his coworkers listen to the phone call morning report of the weirdo's and they seemed to enjoy it.

Neil usually got lost on his daily drive from Hollywood to his apartment in Santa Anita and always called Freddie for directions. One day while he was lost he stopped at a Barbeque place for supper. He called Freddie for directions and when he gave his location to Freddie, he panicked and said "Get back on the Freeway and get to hell out of there, you are in Watts." Neil didn't know about the history of Watts, he never paid attention to skin color and he didn't understand Freddie's concern. He told him OK I will leave as soon as I finish eating my Barbeque. Next day in the morning report they joked that he would risk his life for Barbeque. Neil sensed they were afraid of Black people and he made a mental note.

A few years later Freddie was out of work and Neil fixed him up with a nice paying job for the TVA in West Memphis, Tennessee. West Memphis has a majority black population and a very high crime rate. Freddie lasted a few months because of the crime and when he resigned Neil told him "Do you remember the morning reports in Hollywood, do you remember me risk my life for Barbeque?" Well we are even. Their friendship went on even with them being nothing alike but always respectful.

Neil and Freddie worked one job in Indonesia together. Neil worked in the jungles and Freddie worked in the office and one day Neil took him to the jungles with him. They were driving a jungle road in a small Toyota truck and the road was nothing more than a small cut thru the jungle just big enough for one car to drive down. The sides of the road were swamps and rivers. They stopped at a ferry boat landing and bought hot canned coke colas. As they drove down the road Neil opened his cola and it exploded on to the truck windshield. He didn't stop but he was trying to clean the windshield and was paying little attention to the road. He first heard Freddie scream and when he looked up he saw the face of a male Baboon monkey firmly planted in the windshield with his angry eyes looking directly into Freddie's. The monkey was very dead and had given his life guarding the road crossing for his Harem. Freddie never again rode with Neil to see the jungle. He was traumatized for weeks. Neil was back in the jungle the next day enjoying watching the animals.

The last time they worked together was later in Indonesia and Freddie was having trouble finding a job, Neil got him hired but they worked in different locations. Neil's friend Jos A discovered a pirate town along the East coast of Sumatra that was the "CostCo" of Indonesia. Pirate's raided and robbed ships going thru the Striates of Malaga between Indonesia and Malaysia. They had stores where they sold the stolen goods. Neil was a smoker but could not smoke the clove cigarettes of Indonesia and Marlboro cigarettes were hard to find but they were always available at CostCo Sumatra. The CostCo was out of town and in a valley out of sight. The Indonesians called the community "The Valley of the Dolls." It was operated by an Indonesian Navy Admiral but the houses that were built around the store were like a Mexican "Boys Town" where Indonesian soldiers and Sailors got separated from their money on payday. Girls working there came from all over Indonesia and Malaysia which was a short boat ride away. The town had its own police and security force and for the most part everyone was well behaved but sometimes the girls and guys would have scores to settle. JosA was Neil's work partner and translator and he often got upset because the animals of the jungle had no problem showing themselves to Neil. JosA thought it wasn't normal for wild animals to reveal themselves to anyone. JosA told Neil "I have worked in these jungles for 15 years and I never saw any of these animals alive until you came here. " Neil didn't think of them as wild animals. JosA and Neil stopped by the Valley whenever they were working in the area.

JosA had a brother living in Los Angeles and JosA liked Freddie because of his California weirdness. JosA loved talking to Freddie and was amused by his point of view on life but Neil knew it was always what Freddie did and not what he said that spoke volumes about what he really thought. JosA and Neil invited Freddie to go with them to the Valley of the Dolls. It turned out to be a major mistake.

Neil and JosA always went to the house closest to the Police Station, payed the police to guard the truck and behaved while they were there. The house they went to sold cold beer and had a long front porch where the girls could listen to music, dance and look for customers and hope that their military boy fiends would show up. The house was one of the 57 houses that had rooms for 10 girls and offered fun and entertainment for a price. The sailors and soldiers were there a few days each month before their pay day was spent and promises to pay next payday were made.

JosA knew many of the girls and most of them were runaways hiding from their family. Some were girls who owe money to the Chinese mafia and were trying to pay debt. Some were divorced muslins who could not get pregnant and were desperate to prove it was the husbands fault. JosA had met a girl who came from a poor family and had been raped by a policeman in her hometown. She had scars both inside and outside and feared for her life but JosA was her special boyfriend and he helped her get her body and mind working. JosA was her lover and therapist. JosA had been going to the Valley of the Dolls for a long time. He had a reputation for being a great guy and lover. Two of his old girlfriends had married local government officials and they were happily married. JosA was a respected celebrity in spite of his thick glasses and him being less than 5' tall. At the Valley no one knew the special relationship between JosA and his girlfriend except Neil. She had 2 other girls who protected her at all times. One of the girls was her best friend from her hometown and the other was a runaway daughter from an army officer stationed 100 miles away.

One night Neil and JosA took the girlfriends into town to a nice restaurant. It was Freddie's first trip to the Valley and he didn't want to go with them to town so he stayed in the Valley. Freddie was left in the

Valley in the company of a very quiet runaway who rarely spoke. Her father was in the Army and when he was assigned duty in Sumatra and left their home town in Java she was upset and ran to find shelter in the Valley. Most of her problem was one of her breast was larger than the other one and she was extremely shy. In the weeks that followed it was discovered the girl had been a virgin until Freddie was left alone with her.

The Indonesian man in the Valley who was her boyfriend wanted to kill Freddie and a month later Freddie had found a place for her to live near his work. He had JosA bring her to him without telling Neil. Freddie never told anyone about his deeds but when the Indonesian boyfriend told Neil he was going to kill Freddie Neil told him "Freddie is my best friend I will not allow you to kill him even though what he did was stupid and wrong. So if you want to kill my friend you better kill me first." JosA, Neil and the man drank beer together and it was decided that he would kill Freddie only if he ever saw him again. Case was close and Freddie was banned from ever going back to the Valley.

The girl soon forgot about her friends in the Valley. The girl's name was Fitri. The place where Freddie hid Fitri was an old fashion whorehouse just outside the main gate to their work compound. It was a place where Neil & JosA never went to. She learned all the tricks from watching women sell sex every day. She didn't have to work for a living because Freddie supported her and was with her every day until all hell broke loose. The whorehouse was the safest place for her because it was owned by the Oil Company's chief of security and was managed by his mother in law. It wasn't Fitri's security in question, it was Freddie's.

One of the 25 Americans working for the company had married an Indonesian woman; although she had met her husband in a Red Light district in Jakarta, she had mothered 2 of his children and she had become a Holy Rolling muslin. She didn't like the Americans having girlfriends but she especially didn't like the Americans who lived in the camp with "Subcontracted wives or 2nd wives. These were women and men who had their living together sanctioned by a muslin preacher and were registered with the government authorities.

All hell broke loose when the wife of an employee sent her letters. She managed to get each American's home address from their work records and sent a letter to their wives telling her that her husband was "living in sin." The wives all got the same letter but their reactions became a side show. Some wives first action was to mail her husband divorce papers, some call their husband crying and demanding he come home. Others got an airplane ticket and came to kill the other woman. When Sai got the letter she left the kids with Grandma and came over to see what was going on. Gail called Neil a month later and she was upset about another woman talking about her husband and told Neil with a smile that they would talk about when he got home. Her smiles had disappeared by the time he got home. Every wife handled it different. Their friend Robert who was from Louisiana his wife suddenly showed up and for the next few weeks Robert started buying Viagra by the dozens. The divorces were about 30% after the letter. Freddie went home 3 months later. Neil stayed for 2 more years. Their other friend's wife was from Texas and she called to tell him that she had sold his $50,000 custom built horse trailer and before he went home he said "I will kill her." They remained happily married and the fact that she was a Deputy Sheriff might have helped them reason it out. Everyone wanted to kill the letter writer but life went on. After their Australian friend had finished his divorce he declared the letter a total disaster, a Nuke that leveled the battle field.

Life went on and a year later JosA's girlfriend saved money, started a business in her home town of selling supplies to the new palm oil farmers. er friend H Her girlfriend married a Customs official and was well taken care of for a while. Fitri married a German engineer who worked in Indonesia but her and Freddie would always remain in contact and would have hook ups whenever possible.

Yes there were too many 44 year old memories and secrets to resolve in a mere 1500 mile drive to the funeral.

Now Sai was dead. She had been sick for 4 or 5 years, her liver had failed and she had looked for medical help everywhere, she tried everything but couldn't find anything that worked. Freddie planned the funeral. It was a catered funeral and he called it "A celebration of life" Neil was completely disgusted because he knew it was a very sad day, he could never eat food at a funeral. He knew her children and grandchildren wouldn't feel like eating food and he knew that his friend Freddie would never be the same. Gale was also disgusted until Freddie told her that Sai would be cremated and half of her ashes would be taken back to Thailand and entombed with her mother and Freddie would keep the other half of her ashes at home with him. Gale and Sai had both become Christians but again the differences were great. Sai had joined a Thai church in Los Angeles and Gail had joined a Methodist church while living in Alabama. Sai liked having cook outs and visiting with church members. Gale liked going to church to help old people and children. Gale didn't listen to the preacher she practiced what her parents taught her. Neil knew her early Buddhist teachings were still inside her and she listened to spirits inside the church and not the preachers. Neil didn't forget about Gale and Sai growing up as Buddhist and believing that the cremations were important so the person could be born again and start a new life.

When they went to Gale's family funerals Neil would help sifting thru the cremated ashes of her family member looking for small bones to give to the closest relative. Even Gail didn't understand how he could do that job but to Neil it was just paying respect to the departed. The bones and ashes were just the remains of a loved one.

The monks would spread the cremated remains on a blanket and after the bone fragments were removed, the monk would spread out the ashes and wait for the departed person to leave the ashes and go to their new body. Gail's brother and Neil had cleaned out the bones, spread the ashes and Neil waited to see the new tracks. The monk told Neil the tracks would not appear while he watched. Gail's brother told Neil that the monk was full of crap. He said "people don't return as animals, they either go to heaven or come back as people. Neil watched the ashes at a distance for 2 hours, them he walked back to the ashes and clearly saw new foot prints from a deer. No one had gone near the ashes. Maybe, just maybe the monk was right and the brother in law was wrong. All he knew it was the foot prints of the deer and it was not made by any person. Maybe people did return as animals.

Funny things started happening after Sai died that scared Freddie and their son Pat. The day after she died all the fire alarms went off in the house. Next night after checking the alarms they went off again. Some items in the house seemed to move themselves and noises could be heard coming from her bath room. By the time Neil and Gale drove from Houston to Las Vegas; Freddie and Pat could still feel her presence and were alarmed but they were content with the communications coming from her. Neil listened to their stories but his brain told him the Native American story his Grandmother had told him as a child. "When people pass from this world to the New World they are given 7 days to go where they want to and do what they want to." "They can get even with the people who wronged them, they can talk to loved ones and they can go anywhere in a heartbeat to see things they never got to see." He told Freddie and Pat to "Just give her some space and listen when she talks to them." She did speak to them but she also spoke to Neil and Gale.

Neil, Gale, Freddie and Pat went for breakfast at a casino near their home. As they were leaving Neil put 10 dollars in a slot machine, played for a short time and then cashed out a ticket for $67.87 then walked to the cashier to pay for breakfast. When the cashier told Neil the breakfast bill was $67.87, Neil said "Wow I just won breakfast." Pat went livid and said "She is still messing with us." Neil thought it was just a coincident and told Pat it was just a random event.

They stopped by another casino because Pat had said it was his Mom's favorite one. Neil put a $20 bill in a slot machine as he waited for the others to play slots or go to the bathroom. When he cashed out he got a pay ticket for $88.14 and cashed it in. On the way home they stopped by a gas station to fill up the near empty truck. Neil walked in the gas station as the others stayed in the truck. When Neil returned the gas tank was full and the pump had stopped on $88.14. Neil said nothing but he knew Sai was helping by being generous as she always had been.

Freddie had not set a date for the funeral because some attending had to travel from overseas. Neil decided to call the Tropicana hotel because it was one of the oldest hotels in Las Vegas and easy to get in and out of and it was the hotel where him and Gale had spent their honeymoon 40 years ago. The Tropicana gave them 7 nights' free stay and $170 a day for food. Neil thought it unusual they should be so generous but he did not want to spend another night in Sai's house. It hurt too much to see her things still in place and after Gale told Freddie how to take care of the Persimmon trees that Sai had planted, they moved into the Tropicana. During the night before they had spent it in Sai's house. Neil had a rough dream and Gale tossed and turned in her sleep. The next day neither shared their dreams but Neil's dream was clear. During the night Sai told Neil "I want you to love my oldest daughter as much as I love her." Her oldest daughter's father had abandoned her and ran away with his new love from Germany and she never fit in the family like their other 2 children. She got married very young, had 3 kids of her own, got divorced, was not being supported by her X and she was now living in Los Angeles as a single mother of 3. She was having a hard time making a life for her 3 kids. Neil never liked her X husband even if Freddie and Sai spoke well of him and Sai remained friends with him after the divorce, so he paid little attention to their situation and in his dream he thought "What to hell does she mean, Sai rarely asked favor from anyone in life, why was she doing it from beyond? She was a giver and not a taker." How can I give a mothers love to someone in such a pickle? After the funeral the daughter ran to Neil, cried so hard on his chest that her tears got his shirt wet and he knew exactly what Sai meant.

Gale didn't talk about her dream but 2 weeks after the funeral she went back to her family home in

Thailand to see her family and to visit the graveyard of her mother and stand by the giant vase that held all or her family's ashes so she could talk to them. She didn't talk to Neil much about her need to go visit her family ashes but when Neil called her and she and her sister had completed the graveyard visit and they were sitting along the banks of the mighty Mekong River 600 mile from their home. It was at night and they were watching as fishermen exploded fireworks above the water to cause a great dragon living in the river to appear above the water and breathe his fire towards them; he knew she was ok even though she said she wasn't sure she had actually seen the dragon.

When she told him her exact location, Neil didn't tell her that at that same exact spot on the Mekong 53 years earlier that he had seen boats made from giant teak logs carrying more than 100 men each race up the river for the pride of their village. The boat races were difficult because the boats were heavy and long, the currents were so swift and the race could not start until the 2 boats were side by side. They always raced against the currents and the races were dangerous when the hollowed out teak logs turned sideways to the currents. Neil remembered the beating of the loud drums by the boat master to make sure all rowing efforts were in unison. He also didn't tell her about the American war plane, the Fantom F4 that was shot down in that spot on the river or about the rescue helicopter that was also shot down while recovering the pilot and the plane or the other F4's that bombed the villages into submission. He didn't tell her that his Army buddy who had taken him to see the boat races was now the Chief of his Tribe in New Mexico. He didn't tell her that it was at the Casino of his friend where he won $12,000 and she was afraid to leave the casino for fear of being robbed. He didn't tell her that the healing Sand Pit where he got a final cure for cancer was near his friend's home; the same friend that had sat with him and watched boat racing on the Mekong River. The same spot where her and her sister went to see a fire breathing dragon

He also didn't tell her that at Sai's funeral while he was sitting alone on a bench outside the funeral home door waiting to go inside the funeral home; he heard a noise and looked down under the bench and saw a beautiful black and white fat mouse looking at him and smiling by wiggling her whiskers . He thought "Sometimes there are so many things that are too hard to explain."

Aunt Sai's Advice

Self is a refuge-❀

There is one truth of elderly people.
Who do elderly people have to take care of? Self and self
Have your own body and mind to take good care of.
There are a couple who take care of each other until old.
That's our side person to cherish

We are old and getting old good that the body is good
That's good. The brain is good.

1. When I was 60-70, my body was still good.
If you like to eat anything, eat it.
If you like to wear a beautiful shirt, you can wear it.
If you like to travel anywhere, go to travel.

This time should be prepared to save a part of the money.
Emergency or necessary

Good status. That's good for cuddle terriers cuddle kids.

The child is final. It's good for you.

But don't wait for them to help us

Or wait for him to give me a lot of cuddle.

We have to rely on ourselves very much.

Manage our lives well

2. 70 years old. No disease. It's not a problem.

But I have to know that I'm old and I'm going to have a recession.

Getting older, doing something slow.

Eat slowly because I'm afraid to choke.

Walk slowly because I'm afraid of tripping.

Take care of yourself. Don't mess with kids about grandchildren.

Might look selfish

However, I have to take care of my health. Because not relying on others is great.

3. When the body is not good, you need to prepare
yourself to accept the pain
the old and the dead are coming.

Don't be too burdened to pass the final.
Of life when life is decadent both brain and body.
Face your face with death.
Don't let sickness be a burden to pay.
Last session in massive amount unnecessarily
effort to hold life to survive

Don't forget that the most important thing is
"self is a refuge"
The descendants of relatives are the fillers.

[Aunt Sai's assistant]

SOMETIMES I LAUGH TO KEEP FROM CRYING

The army kept its promise to give Neil an adventure. In 1966, the Vietnam War was heating up. It seemed the world had chosen sides in Vietnam's civil war. The Russians and other communist countries were supporting the North, and America and its allies were supporting the South. The war had escalated, with each supporting side providing military advisors, weapons, and soldiers. In the beginning, the North was not led by a communist but by a patriot who had witnessed the inhuman practices of the colonial rule enforced during the French colonial period. It was a period when the Vietnamese were used for slave labor and had no say in the rule of their own country. The patriot had traveled the globe and once worked as a pastry chef at a Hilton hotel. The patriot's love for his country and his people could never be questioned. His Chinese ethnicity was questioned because China had previously colonized Vietnam and he was Chinese. The South was led by a man who was strong in his Catholic religion, even though 95 percent of the country claimed and practiced the Buddhist religion. America had just elected their first Catholic president, and he fully supported the Catholic-ruled South. No one was willing to compromise, and the war grew. The peace-loving Buddhist monks were protesting by burning themselves to death in public places. The news media had grown with its use of satellite television, film, and telephone communications. Each day, the entire world could hear and watch the war.

When the cost of the war escalated beyond America's budgets and the American Catholic president was murdered, America decided we had to win this war. The Soviets decided they could not allow America to win. More weapons and troops were needed to win. America had a Selective Service system for drafting men to serve in the military. Each male over eighteen years old was eligible, but it allowed for draft exemptions. Until 1966, most of the draft requirements were filled by volunteers. One of the draft exemptions was for students attending college.

A few years earlier, America and Russia had discovered how to reach into space with rockets and people. This required engineers and scientists, so they changed the military draft exemptions to allow education exemptions for only those in college who studied science or engineering. This made 80 percent of college students eligible for the military draft, and the Selective Service offices started sending out letters saying, "Report to … and be prepared for," all prefaced by "if you fail to do so, you will go to jail." Protests started with college students burning their draft cards and letters. Some moved to Canada, and protests were shown on the nightly news. The president used the National Guard to battle the protestors, but after the National Guard used live bullets on student protestors, everything changed. The protests grew until they were considered counterculture. The protestors had their own revolution, complete with music, drugs of choice, and legal and monetary support. It seemed the world had been watching, and the students had also been watching how government officials found ways to get exemptions to the draft for their own children.

It was a time when eighteen-year-olds had to decide for themselves. The choices were not easy and would be lifelong.

Neil was confused about going into the military, as were all his friends. His brother Joe had been in the army since he was seventeen years old, and by the time he was twenty-two, he was a helicopter pilot flying gunships. He enjoyed being in the army. When he wasn't in Vietnam or some other hot spot, he flew either mapping the western states or training new helicopter pilots. Joe had exceptional vision and viewed his job as just putting on a helicopter and going hunting. He had always been a great hunter, and being in the army was a job he loved. Neil did not understand why people did not want to serve in the military. His father had served, his uncles had served, and both sides of the family had served during the Civil War. His family had served in every American war. Some had served in the American Revolution. He concluded that it was his duty to serve if he was called, and he would do so. He did not want to serve in a peacetime army, but if Americans were getting killed in a war, he would definitely serve, because it was his duty to his family. The press wasn't calling

Vietnam a war. No declaration of war had been made, and he thought maybe it would all just go away. It was just a conflict, but they had said the Korean War was just a "police action." He remembered looking out the school bus window on every trip to school and seeing his neighbor Mr. Lankford carrying flowers to the grave of his son who had been killed in the police action.

Neil and his two friends, Gerald and Gene, were working for the Texas prison system. The state of Texas had hired a new director for their prison system, a Methodist minister who was tasked with reforming the fully segregated system into a modern, humane system where every convict would be given a chance to reform. He hired the young and inexperienced to replace the older guardians. He coined a saying that defined his beliefs, "Prisons are to confine the punished, not to punish the confined." Some people strongly objected to the new system, with the focus on rehabilitation, but proof that it worked was measured by the recidivism of convicts. In 1966, the Texas prisons were segregated by race and offense. The new director gave directives that required all officers to spend two hours each week reading the court records and prison files of the convicts they were supervising. Neil didn't enjoy the reading at first, but each file seemed to tell a story and gave an identity to the convict. It made them a person and not just a number.

The 1960s had America working in three important challenges that would forever change America. Civil rights needed to be defined by law and fixed so all people could be treated as equals. States had made their own laws, and they prevailed for centuries because the federal government didn't have specific laws that overruled the state laws. Before the federal authorities made laws, the inequity of law filled the states' rulings, and each state had different laws. Some states had laws defining use of public water fountains, seating on public transportation, and segregated schools based on race. All these state laws used ethnicity, race, and skin color of a person to determine legality and jurisdiction. It had to be fixed, but the feds moved slowly. It seemed that the federal lawmakers had trouble defining the rights of men and women, because fifty years earlier, women were fighting for their rights. Eventually, they passed laws for all men and women, but the laws did not include all people who identified as either man or woman.

The space age had started for control of the planet. New technology allowed space exploration and military superiority in the Cold War as communism of the Soviet Union battled with democracy of America and the free world. Atomic weapons grew in number until they were so plentiful on both sides that neither could destroy the other without destroying themselves. The tired old European monarchs were desperately trying to rebuild to their former glory of planet rule after WWII, because during WWII, they had been almost destroyed. They constantly touted the Soviets and Americans as being each other's enemy. America and Russia paid to rebuild their countries, but they were not friends with either Russia or America. Brush fires had to be put out in every corner of the globe as Europeans tried to find new ways to recolonize and rob the developing countries of resources to enrich their ancient societies. To Neil, it seemed like a schoolyard fight with some ten-year-old boys squaring off face-to-face, an agitator boy putting his finger in front of their faces and saying, "First man who spits over my finger is the best man." One of them spits, and the war starts. Civil rights and the race to the moon were shadowed by the conflict in Vietnam.

Neil, Gerald, and Gene worked at the prison at night and carpooled to the nearest college, where the studied to advance themselves, have a social life outside of the prison, and avoid the military draft. Neil studied every subject that ended in *ology*—sociology, psychology, criminology, penology—law, and history. He had learned that some very good men would spend their entire lives in prison, and he was looking for answers. He cared nothing about being awarded a degree; he really believed some of the condemned could be made whole and reformed. Gene had a plan to get his bachelor's degree and become a teacher who could teach children to stay out of prison. Gerald studied girls and enrolled in classes that had the most girls. They all received their draft letters at the end of summer classes and started making other plans. The army was about to change their lives. Neil and Gerald resigned from their jobs at the prison. Gene visited an army recruiter and continued working at the prison until he went into the army. The summer soon ended, and they all went on to serve in the army.

The army recruiter told Gene that his best option was to join the army and request a specific assignment. Gene wanted to gain college credits while he served in the army, so the recruiter offered a career for him. He could go to the Defense Language Institute, and after completion, he would be assigned to a foreign embassy as a foreign language specialist. When Gene explained this to Neil and Gerald, he said that to qualify, you had to join the army for four years; the time required if you were drafted was two years. Gerald said, "I know that four is twice as long as two, so I am definitely not joining." Neil said he needed to think about it. Neil and Gerald got jobs working for a pipeline company in Louisiana. The pay was fifteen times better than the ten-dollar-a-day prison pay, and during their last four months of work, they could save money for when they went into the army. The four months passed quickly, and their reporting day was set for the first day of September.

Neil had worked as a radiographer before working at the prison and had received his license. When he was hired by the pipeline company, he hired Gerald and a friend from his hometown to be his helpers. His friend Kenneth was recently divorced and needed a change of scenery for a few months. Kenneth was small in stature but tough and tempered. He would fight anyone at the drop of a hat, and it didn't seem to matter that he rarely won a fight.

The pipeline work was twelve hours long and seven days a week. It kept them busy and out of trouble—until they were working on a pipeline that ran under the Red River. The contractor bored a tunnel under the river and pushed the pipe casing in the tunnel, but there were lots of delays. The pipeline had to be deep enough to keep the river's barge traffic from ripping it out. The contractor couldn't get it right, so they had a week of doing nothing except waiting. They got bored, and the boredom led to their first military experience. They lived and worked out of the town of Alexander. It was a large river town and home to an important US Air Force base. They could hear the airplanes flying the skies around Alexander as they practiced to go to war. Neil and the crew paid no attention to the air base until one night when they stopped at a bar for a beer and relief from hours of waiting for the contractor to complete the Red River pipeline crossing.

They went in the bar not knowing anyone but came out knowing everyone. In the bar, they met an old friend from their hometown, and he bought them round after round of beer as he told his story. He had impregnated his girlfriend. His father made him quit high school and get married, and then he started working for his father's plastering company full-time. He had been hanging sheetrock since he was twelve years old and had mastered the trade. His father's company was having a hard time, so he had come to Alexander to start his own company, and the rapidly expanding air base was his best customer. He had done well by being at the right place at the right time.

His story lasted too long and required drinking too many free beers. At some point during the storytelling, the bar filled up with airmen from the local base. Then exotic dancers appeared on stage. The storytelling stopped when the dancing started. The strippers kept the crowd entertained, and when two strippers started making out on the stage, things got tense. One of the strippers had an orgasm and lay down on the stage as the other stripper stood over her and poured a cold beer on her to revive her. After this part of the show, a couple air force policemen appeared, and the lights came on. It was time for everyone to go home, and everyone knew it except the pipe liners.

One of the air force policemen was a large, fat man with thick glasses. He tried to remove the girls, but one of the strippers took off his glasses. He stumbled around the stage, trying to find the girls, as the other airmen laughed. The stripper who poured the beer sat down at their table, holding his glasses. She told Kenneth it was all a part of the act, but Kenneth was mad because the beer she had poured on the orgasm-convulsing girl was Kenneth's beer, and she was disrespecting a man in uniform. He slapped her and said, "Give me the damn glasses." Then he walked on stage and handed the glasses to the blind air force cop. Kenneth respected all men in uniform, but that was not fully understood, as the entire club erupted into a fight—with Kenneth being the focus.

The fight moved outside the bar to the parking lot and turned into a drunk free-for-all. Some airmen were fighting with other airmen, but Kenneth led the charge. Gerald and Neil threw a few defensive punches but mostly watched as Kenneth attached himself to the head of a very large airman and constantly hit him in the face. The airman dropped to the asphalt and twisted his head, with Kenneth attached. It reminded Neil of seeing a raccoon attacking a bloodhound, and it was almost funny. The sound of police sirens grew loud, and everyone went home.

For the crew, home was an old motel a few miles from the bar. They made it home safely, and all was well for a half hour until Kenneth realized the extent of his injuries. Gerald said, "We need to take him to the hospital," because the asphalt had torn out chunks of flesh from his arms and back.

Neil was mad at Kenneth for starting the fight, and he told Gerald to get the first aid kit out of the work truck and doctor him up. "When he sobers up, he'll be fine."

Kenneth screamed as Gerald doctored him from the first aid kit.

The next morning, Gerald said, "We really need to take Kenneth to a hospital. You've got to see this." Kenneth's fifty-plus wounds on his arms and back from the scratches of the asphalt had blister bags full of clear liquid hanging from them. Neil told Gerald to show him what medicine he had used to doctor Kenneth's wounds. Iodine was the common treatment for cuts and scratches, and each first aid kit had a bottle of iodine. The bottle Gerald used was labeled "Corn Remover." They carried Kenneth to the hospital, missed half a day of work, and received a call from the boss in Dallas saying that they were all fired for missing work.

The morning had been busy and eventful. Neil spent the afternoon in the army recruiter's office, trying to remember what Gene had said to him about the Defense Foreign Language Institute. The next day, Neil was on a bus going to Shreveport for processing into the army. Gerald was on his way to Dallas to drop off the work truck and get his last paycheck. Kenneth was going home. The summer was turning into fall, and the daylight hours were getting shorter.

The army bus was full of new recruits as it left Shreveport, heading north through the Arkansas Ozark Mountains. It went through towns that Neil had never heard of. It stopped for fuel a few times and drove on to Fort Leonard Wood, Missouri. One of the other army recruits said, "Now I know why they call this place Fort Lost in the Woods." Basic training started as soon as the bus stopped.

The first week in the army included lots of screaming by the army training personnel. Everyone got army uniforms and haircuts so everyone looked the same. Most of the screaming was about staying in line while marching, not talking, and not even looking around. Mostly, the first week was about being tested in a classroom. Many physical and mental tests had to be taken, and all tests were taken in complete silence. There were forms with questions about your family history, a list of your friends, and a list of skill sets and licenses in your name. Each day also included physical exercises and reading a small book on the soldiers' code of conduct.

After a week of processing and testing, they started learning to run, jump, and shoot. Delta Company had a few rules that the other companies didn't have. Before each meal, the recruits had to swing their bodies down twenty yards of monkey bars; if you fell off, you went to the end of the line, and those who couldn't swing their way to the mess hall ate last. Each recruit ran a mile before breakfast and a mile before going to bed. The ten men who finished last had to run another mile. Neil thought that these were army rules, but they were not; they were the rules for Delta Company. Neil had no trouble with the monkey bars, but running was a problem because the entire company ran faster each day and night. He learned to run by thinking about his first girlfriend;

his breathing was controlled as he thought of kissing her. It worked, and he never finished last, and in their last company run before completing basic training, he finished first. The weapons' training was easy because he had been shooting guns since his sixth birthday. In three months, he was ready to be trained as a soldier. His body was ready, so now the army would train his brain.

Gene was in a company across the base and on the same time table, so Neil and Gene flew home together. Gerald was at a base in Texas, training to be a combat medic. Neither Neil nor Gene knew what they were going to be, because the promise made by the army recruiter was totally dependent on the security clearance level. When they got home, their friends and family told them that the FBI had been asking questions about them. They would learn their fate sometime next year after the investigations.

The next year, they learned they both had been accepted to the Defense Language Institute. Gene was going to study Chinese, and Neil was going to study Vietnamese. They were both going to be stationed at Fort Devens, just outside Boston. Then they were going to Monterrey, California. Gene's training would require eighteen months, and Neil's required only six months. Neil had had no intention to learn to speak, read, and write Vietnamese. He didn't even know that Vietnamese was a language, so during the additional testing at Devens, the army decided he qualified for the very highest security clearance the army gave. They would give him a new job, but they explained that if he ever told anyone about his new job, he would go directly to jail. He never told anyone about his new job. He trained for his new job for fourteen months and then was assigned to a base in Bavaria, Germany. During WWII, the base had been the German Air Force Academy, and every German pilot in WWII lived and trained at that base. Now he would do his new job inside the old airplane hangars.

Gene finished his training and was assigned to Okinawa. He put his language skills to use. Gerald completed his medical training and was sent to an army base in Korea. The biggest part of his duties was giving local hookers pap smears so they could be issued a VD-free card to work in the bars just outside the base. It seemed his interest in women had been duly noticed by the army during his training.

The army didn't require Neil to wear a uniform to work, and at some point, they gave him a red diplomatic passport. They told him not to use it but to keep it with him whenever he traveled. The job was very interesting, and the name "Special Operations" had little meaning because he had never served a day with the regular army. The same army general had remained at the top of his chain of command since his first day in the army, and he thought it odd that the general seemed to be following him.

The off-duty travel in Germany was mostly driving through and around the Alp Mountains and visiting wartime places like the concentration/extermination camps and military graveyards. He also went to the home base and training base of the German Gestapo, the beer hall where Hitler made his first speech, the church where an American paratrooper hung from the steeple and was killed by Germans, and the town where General Patton executed fifty Germans for killing the American paratrooper. Hitler's Eagle Nest offered some strange insight as an ideal resting and relaxing place, but it seemed to have much blood on the stones, and Ludwig's castle, which was copied for Walt Disney, seemed to say, "Yes, Ludwig was really into magic mushrooms." It seemed surreal that all these things happened in Bavaria, one of the most beautiful places on earth. The old church where Martin Luther posted his call for church reform seemed to have some magic when one touched the nail holes where he posted his thesis on the church door. Most of all, Neil enjoyed reading the copy of General Patton's diary that he found in the base library. The diary explained how a war was won, his love of soldiers, and his hate of enemies. Neil learned exactly how and when his favorite uncle had earned the steel plate in his head while serving as a personal soldier for General Patton.

The Germans seemed to be a hardworking people who really enjoyed their beer halls. It seemed odd that most of the older Germans often said that during WWII was the best time of their lives. Neil didn't understand how a war could be anything but pure horror, because his uncles' stories had expressed surviving in hell. One of his uncles had been awarded five Bronze Stars while serving in Germany, and the only funny stories that he, Neil's father, and Neil's other uncles ever told were about exchanging chocolate bars for sex and using their army C rations to feed starving Germans.

The fun part of being in the army ended for Neil when his cousin, after being drafted and going through three months of training, was sent directly to Vietnam, where he was killed during his first month of service. Billy Mac was like a little brother, and his being killed in action hit hard. With a heavy heart, Neil spoke to his commander and told him he wanted to go to Vietnam. His brother Joe did the same thing. They both felt guilty that Billy Mac got killed, because the lost look on his parents' faces seem to speak to them about honor and duty. Joe had already served two tours in Vietnam and knew what to expect, but Neil had no idea what was about to happen. The army had promised him an adventure, but he didn't expect it to be so gut-wrenchingly personal. Maybe he should have gone to the Defense Language Institute. He was a fully trained soldier, and family honor was at stake. but he could only see Billy Mac as a child; he was four years younger and had always been a little brother. He wished he had been with him in Vietnam. He wished he could have saved him. He wished there was no war where American soldiers were being killed, but reality told him get on board and that nothing could keep him from coming home to his two children and wife.

The army did not allow brothers to be in Vietnam at the same time, so they both lied to the army and demanded the army send them. Neither Joe nor Neil knew how to hate anyone or anything, and they would never learn to hate, but family honor and duty spoke volumes to them, and they listened. Maybe it was simply the Native American Indian blood that ran through their veins that told them they were warriors. When Neil asked Joe what war was really like, Joe told him he didn't like it because hunting and killing people was "just too damn easy." One year later, they both came home. During the year, they had learned that being the hunter is a lot safer than being hunted.

The year 1969 ended, and the seventies began. The American government had finally passed some new federal laws as guidelines in response to social inequities. Americans wanted the war in Vietnam to end, and America had sent a man to the moon and brought him back home safely. The Cold War with the Soviet Union was winding down because the communists had watched for fifteen years as American kids became stone-cold killers, and they decided they wanted no part of a land war with America. It was time for these kids to move on.

When Joe and Neil told Billy Mac's parents, "We know how much you hurt when he was killed, and we know how much you suffered, but we can tell you that we have made sure that a lot of Vietnamese parents know exactly how you feel," they both looked puzzled. Neil and Joe learned that being a warrior is a lot easier than not being a warrior, but neither of them had any regrets. They both hid in education and hard work until the war demons abandoned them. It took them a few years to learn that being a soldier never changes, but reactions can be controlled. Neil loved being in the army, but he often said, "They spent hundreds of thousands dollars making me a soldier, but they never spent a damn penny unmaking me."

The trips to the Veterans Administration didn't start until their careers ended and they were retired from work. They learned to live with their wounds of war, and their trips to the VA were not so much for treatment, but when American soldiers started coming back from Iraq and Afghanistan, they wanted to help the new soldiers get the help they needed. Their eyes lit up when they spoke about being soldiers. Kids coming back without arms and legs made them cry like they had never cried before. They wanted to help and get help for the new vets. It seemed strange that they wanted to help, because when they returned from Vietnam, they didn't get any help from the VA. The Vietnam veterans coined a saying that they all understood. "Never again will a generation of American soldiers be forgotten." It was also a duty, and Neil remembered his first trip to the VA in 1970. He had spent his last two months in an army field hospital, learning to walk. The VA sent him a letter telling him he was classified as a "disabled veteran" and that he had to report to the VA for evaluation. He refused to accept that he was a disabled veteran in spite of not being able to walk very well, ride a horse, or swing an ax. The first trip didn't go well. The interview turned south when Neil was sent to the VA quiet room for threatening the doctor who appeared to be uninterested and uncaring. In the quiet room, a WWII vet told him that Vietnam vets were losers because the war was lost. In a steady voice, he told the WWII vet that the final score was 3,500,000 killed to 58,427 killed. How the hell was that losing? The quiet room suddenly got really quiet, but it ended well when the man in charge of the room identified himself as a Vietnam vet. They spoke openly but quietly about being spit on by the war protestors, about Jane Fonda, and about the three US senators who made the rules of war that left American soldiers fighting with one hand tied behind their backs.

The WWII vet watched and listened, and he noticed that one of them was white and one of them was black. The WWII vet seemed confused because Vietnam vets refused to recognize color as having any importance as they looked each other in the eyes and spoke from the heart.

It would take thirty years before Neil went back to the VA, because no help was available there, but now these new soldiers needed help, and he would go there to help them. It took Joe longer. He was retired from the army, and when he or one of his friends would dummy up some old army orders, telling the others that they had been called back to active duty, they seemed to really want the orders to be real.

Neil thought the loss of legs was horrible, but he noticed the new vets seemed to wear the fake legs as a symbol. They could walk and run with the fake legs. As he walked down the VA halls, he noticed a vet in a wheelchair, with his fake leg sticking out the side. He was waiting for repairs as he talked to other vets. The leg had a cup on top where his upper leg fit in. When Neil noticed that it looked like a trophy, he asked the vet if anyone was putting money or trash into his fake leg. He said, "I hope not, because on New Year's, I am going to use it for drinking beer." The surrounding vets laughed. When Neil was setting on a bench waiting for the valet service to bring his truck, he saw another vet in a wheelchair, with his fake leg standing up beside him. The vet was very tall and not very good with a wheelchair, but he was going very fast because he was pulling himself with his good leg and using the push wheels for guiding the direction while crossing the hospital entrance. The valet drivers were being inconsiderate, as if they were being paid by the car. Neil knew most of the drivers because he spoke enough Arabic to talk to them. They were all refugees from Iraq, Syria, or Afghanistan, plus a few Kurds. The first time he saw them, he got upset, thinking it was totally insensitive to the new vets, but his Arabic language skills allowed some understanding of their refugee status.

At the hospital entrance, waiting for his truck to be delivered by the valet, Neil sat on a concrete bench next to a vet who was in quiet mode. Neil said, "That guy has that wheelchair going twenty miles per hour with his one leg. It must be the VA's day to fix fake legs."

The quiet vet pulled up his trouser leg, showed his fake leg, and said, "They need to take better care."

After a doctor visit, Neil stopped by the kiosk that sold military hats. Raj sold the hats, and few people knew that Raj was from India. He had come to America during the sixties and overstayed his visa. Rather than return to India, he joined the US Army and served in an armor division that spent time in Vietnam. Raj came back to Texas as a disabled veteran and ended up selling hats inside the VA hospital. He was soft-spoken and had a head full of things he was trying to resolve. Neil had known him and bought hats from him for years. In the early days, the hats were made in America, but over the years, the hats of the day were all made in Vietnam. Neil was out of the army thirty years before he ever wore a Vietnam hat. Two other Vietnam brothers stood looking at the hats. Most of the hats were for Gulf War veterans, and the Vietnam hats were moved lower in the display. One of the vets was a heavyset black brother who was wearing a hat with the First Air Calvary emblem. The second brother was of Mexican heritage but spoke with a distinct Houston, Texas, accent. Neil was pretty sure he had never been to Mexico, and he was wearing a hat with the Big Red 1 emblem. Neil's brother had served with the First Air Calvary, and they all wore it with pride and distinction. As they looked at the hats, a VA doctor came running down the hallway and then stopped to allow the three policemen following her to catch up.

One of the policemen asked her, "What color is he?"

Neil went ballistic and shouted into the policeman's face, "WTF does it matter what color he is?"

The policeman turned toward Neil but said nothing because the First Air Calvary brother moved between them and said to Neil, "They are just trying to identify him."

The Big Red 1 brother said, "They have to identify him because they need to choose the right weapon to handle the situation."

Raj said, "Yes, if he is black, they will use a Taser. If he is Mexican, they will use a nightstick. If he is white, they will use a gun. All others will get checked for a green card." The four amigos laughed so hard the situation was defused, and no one paid attention to just another vet going crazy.

On the drive home, Neil felt tears running down his cheeks as he thought, *Sometimes you really do have to laugh to keep from crying.*

COLOR-BLIND

I t was six o'clock in the morning, and the casino was almost empty. Speedy had been awake since four in the morning and was on his way to breakfast when he walked by the craps table. Craps was his favorite game, and he stopped to watch. Most of the ten players had spent the entire night standing in one spot, betting and watching as the chips changed to and from the dealers. He noticed the player to his right was betting $500 chips, and he was betting the "don't win" line. All others were betting five-dollar to twenty-five-dollar chips and betting to win. The dice had been cold and unwilling to allow anyone to roll a winning number, and the $500 don't-win chips were winning.

Craps are a funny game because you can win by losing. Speedy knew that the small cubes with numbers from one to six had a mind and a pattern of their own. You had to read the dice as either being hot, cold, or warm. Warm dice produced few winners, but with hot or cold, you could win money. The rules to craps are simple. Roll a seven or eleven on the initial roll, and you win. Roll a two, three, or twelve, and you lose. If you roll another number of four, five, six, eight, nine, or ten, you must roll it again before you roll a seven. Roll a seven after you rolled your first number, and you lose. Roll the same number again, and you win. The green felt craps table is covered with one-time numbers that pay odds. One-time numbers pay from 15:1 up to 30:1. That's the part of craps that makes psyches from ordinary players.

Speedy had no fondness for gambling because the odds of winning are always on the casino's side, but to Speedy, crap dice seemed to be a game of energy and spirits. Everyone knew that if you said, "Tenaha, Timpson, Bobo, and Blair," the next roll of the dice would be a double five, or as crap shooters said, "A hard ten." The supposed random rolls of dice seemed to produce not so random results. Professional crap players call it "reading the dice" and observing if the dice are producing winning numbers or losing numbers and the times when rolling a seven seems impossible. All crap shooters think they are psychics. As Speedy watched, he felt his hand reach for his wallet. He opened his wallet and thought, *This might be a $200 breakfast*, as he bought $200 of casino chips.

The players never speak to one another when the dice are hot and the winners are winning; they are all envisioning the results of their bets and the number of the next roll and making sure their odds bets are being paid correctly. It's a code of conduct that is enforced by the players but not so much by the dealers, because the dealers are watching the table for cheaters—cheaters who hold the dice wrong, touch the dice with both hands, roll the dice incorrectly, or pick up others' betting chips. Craps requires the full attention of players and dealers.

Standing to the right of Speedy was the $500-chip bettor, and to the left was a five-dollar bettor. Speedy usually wore his lucky Vietnam veteran hat to the casino, and he noticed that seven of the ten players were also wearing their lucky Vietnam veteran hats. He thought it unusual because most Vietnam veterans don't like to be recognized and addressed by people who say, "Thank you for your service," because for too many years they had been called "baby-killing losers," and the sting never completely went away. No Vietnam veteran wore a hat for thirty years. Today they are recognized as the best soldiers America ever produced, but the disrespect they suffered still hurt. They all knew the courage and bravery it took to raise their right hand and offer their life to defend our country, and they knew the courage it took to offer their life for a fellow soldier's life. Most of all, they did not feel ill for those who didn't have this bravery and courage to become a soldier. Speedy thought it wasn't so much the bravery as it was the family warrior genes rising to the top, and he had learned that warriors come in all different sizes and shapes. He had seen a fellow warrior start his military career when he was one hundred pounds overweight and could not do one push-up or pull-up. He was made to carry a hundred-pound log with him whenever he was not training. He carried the log with him every day for three months. He had been an intellectual who had a doctorate degree in chemical engineering when he joined the army, but he didn't have a warrior body until he made one. Vietnam veterans had few heroes, but as the years passed, they learned to love one another as their heroes. He looked at their hats and felt at home at the craps table.

When the winning numbers were being rolled and the dealers were slowing down the game by picking up and stacking chips, Speedy turned to the Vietnam vet on his left side. He asked him if he was from Houston, and the man replied, "No. I am from Mississippi." Speedy told him that he had once lived in Mississippi; the town's name was Cleveland. The man got excited and said, "That's my hometown." They talked about the town and life sixty years ago living in the Delta. The man said he had spent most of his life in the army, but upon retirement, he had moved back home. Speedy mentioned that he got in trouble in a casino near his hometown for talking about the Delta. He was playing cards, and the dealer was an old man. When Speedy asked the old man if he ever picked cotton on the grounds where the casino was built, Speedy's friend stood up and walked away but not before he said, "I can't believe you said that."

The dealer smiled and asked Speedy, "Why did you ask that question?"

Speedy said, "It was because when I worked on pipelines, we built one that ran near this casino, and while they were building the pipeline, there was nothing on the land except cotton fields that ran as far as one could see. The air had cotton fibers in it, and the people who worked outside had cotton fibers in their hair. The towns were very poor, and 80 percent of the people worked in the cotton fields."

The old man laughed and said, "Yes, I did pick cotton where this casino sits." The old man spoke with eloquence and grace, and a new friend had been made.

When Speedy told the story to the crap-playing vet, he noticed that the vet was a black man. He told the vet that no one was teaching their children and grandchildren about how tough life used to be in the Delta. The vet responded by telling him that the children and grandchildren really didn't care. It seemed that some of the results of MLK marches through the Delta got good results because his kids and my kids truly don't know or care what price was paid for their freedoms from oppression.

During the next break, the player betting $500 chips turned to Speedy and said, "I really do respect vets. Do either of you have any retirement advice for me? Because I am nearing retirement, and the price of everything keeps going up."

Speedy said, "I can tell you what my grandfather told me when I was ten years old. The first time I repeated it, I got my butt whipped by my father for using cuss words, so don't be offended. Grandfather said, 'Never work for the government—any government—and never owe any sum bitch nothing.'" The crap game came to a halt as the ever-watchful dealers cracked up laughing, and all the other vets thought it so funny they didn't make any bets. The $500-chip bettor looked like he knew what his retirement plans were. He must have known a lot of sum bitches. After the craps game restarted, the breakfast ended up costing Speedy $200, but he remembered holding $750 worth of chips in his hand before the talking began and thinking, *I really need to eat breakfast*, but all he could focus on was, *Why didn't I notice the veteran was a black man?*

LABELS-SAUDI DUST BOWL

The 1990s were an interesting time for work. Al accepted the work assignments that paid the most money. Normally the work assignments included working in remote places that included jungles or deserts. Indonesia, Papua New Guinea, and Saudi Arabia were familiar places for work adventures because they paid more, and while Al's coworkers sometimes referred to themselves as oil field trash whores, Al thought of himself as being a trained monkey chasing money. It was very difficult to spend all the money that he made because in the places he worked, there was nothing to purchase, and he enforced a work rule that said no matter what was happening at work, he would go back to his Texas home every ninety days. If the company did not go along with his rule, he would find another company. Usually he worked with the same people and for the same companies.

Twenty years of overseas work had earned him the label of expatriate, and his expatriate friends were his coworkers. They were all focused on results. The results included developing natural resources and making money for the companies, developing a third world country, and creating jobs for the local people. This was their way of helping people who couldn't help themselves, and it put a happy face on everyone involved. The expatriates worked as a team, and they depended on one another to find jobs and do jobs. They trusted one another. Most of them were experts in their field, and training foreign nationals was a big part of their work. All of the expatriates were uncompromising American patriots, but rarely did they discuss politics or religion with anyone. They did this to show respect for the local people and their fellow workers.

Most people in Papua New Guinea told stories about their grandfathers being cannibals, most Indonesians believed in black magic, and most Saudis practiced their religion without any thought as to why. At certain times of day, they would all stop work and go pray because nothing was more important to them than singing their prayers. Al would forever remember seeing a single camel rider navigating the sand dunes, and at a precise time, he would get off his camel and say his prayers directly to God. Most expatriates said their daily prayers but in silence, and a mutual respect was understood by all.

The expatriates were of all citizenships, but the majority were from America or the United Kingdom. The British were a funny bunch because they all spoke with the dialect of their hometown. The dialects were different even if their hometowns were only twenty miles apart. Most American expatriates spoke with their own dialects and not dialects from their hometown or state; most of them spoke with a Canadian accent.

The men who could work successfully overseas as expatriates were soon labeled by the hiring companies. They sought them for overseas work but ignored them for domestic work because of their label. Al didn't mind overseas work because his ex-wife had moved on to greener pastures, his children were being raised by their grandparents, and his extra money more than supported their expenses. The fact that his ex-wife had moved on three times did bother him, and he didn't trust his reactions to keep himself out of jail. He had become his family's banker, but he knew what his military reactions would be if he witnessed his children going through three ex-stepfathers. He came home four times a year and spent time with his children, going on vacation to any place they wanted to go. The premium overseas pay seemed well spent, and the children seemed to enjoy traveling and getting away from ex-stepfathers.

Bill was a high-tech computer jockey. His job was to make sure all computers were working and all data was securely stored for future use that defined the use of resources. Most overseas projects were not well defined, except for top-level economics and social impacts. It was important to define actual requirements of money, equipment, and manpower being used to complete the projects. The importance was to justify project economics and improve the planning of future development programs. The world banks were eager to finance developing countries but only if they could make money. Computers were an absolute necessity for capturing all the data, and Bill had experience with big computers. The company hired him to keep the computers running and safely store the mountains of data. The project was simple. The Saudi oil companies had been flaring gas to the atmosphere in order to produce their ten million barrels of oil. The flare had grown so large that it could be seen from the moon. A university in America had envisioned using the gas to create industries and sold their ideas to the Saudis and the World Bank. The gas would be captured and used to create other industries. The industries would be fertilizer and plastics.

A team of expatriates was formed to do the job. It would be challenging. The expatriate labor force included more than ten thousand men, and they came from twenty-two different countries. The management was mostly Americans and British but with others from Europe and South America. The laborers were mostly from Indonesia, Turkey, and Korea. To accommodate the ten-thousand-man workforce, the company had built a camp in the middle of the Saudi desert. The camp included cafeterias for the different nationalities, indoor and outdoor movie theaters, and soccer fields and baseball fields that were also used for cricket. The camp was a very diverse city. The camp had no telephones or any way to communicate with the outside world—except for driving forty miles to the nearest city and using a telephone guarded by the Saudi military. Bill was confused by the remoteness and diversity of the project. He was also confused by the ever-changing challenges and evolution to smaller and more powerful computers.

Bill earned the label of being a computer nerd, and he relished it, but he never earned the label of being an expatriate. The remoteness of the job location and lack of telephones soon overpowered him, and he had a meltdown. The center of the camp had a soccer field. The lights stayed on twenty-four hours a day because the sports fields were without a means to turn off the lights. The switching gear had not been delivered; it was not a job priority, and it provided security. The lights burned twenty-four hours a day.

Bill took everything out of his room and moved it to center field of the baseball grounds. When his coworkers spotted him, they approached him and questioned him. He said he was confused in his room and wanted to sort things out. He felt comfortable being in center field because it had the best view of the game. He said he had sorted everything by color and then by age, but nothing seemed to be sorted out correctly. They gave him a hug and said they would help, but they needed to take it all back to his room. He agreed, and they took him back to his room, helped him organize his belongings, and spent the rest of the night talking to him about going home for a while.

Bill was not from Houston. His parents were divorced, with his mother living in San Antione and his father was living in Las Vegas. Bill said he needed to see a doctor, but he didn't know any in Houston. Neil told him that his mother was a nurse at the largest hospital in Houston and she would help him find the right doctor. The next day, Bill was on his way home, with an escort to travel with him to the hospital.

A few months later, Neil went home and learned that his mother had sent Bill to the correct doctor and that Bill was still in a hospital. He went to see him. Bill welcomed him and told him that he was fine, except he had suffered a reaction to medication. While he was explaining his medical problems, a nurse came in and told Bill she had contacted an insect exterminator and he would be there shortly. After the nurse left the room, Neil asked Bill what kind of insects were in the hospital. Bill said he had seen ants crawling up the window. Neil responded by saying, "Bill, we are on the twentieth floor. It must be some really strong ants that are unafraid of heights." They then talked about the work in Saudi, and Bill seemed normal and laughed when Neil told him that his old boss wife left him and ran away with a Catholic priest.

When Neil went to see his parents, his mother told him that Bill's main problem was he was gay. Neil was shocked because that was not what he expected to hear. Neil always tried to stay away from things he didn't understand, and his only experience with anyone being gay was his uncle's prized bull. His uncle had paid top dollar for a beautiful bull to improve his cattle herd, but after a year, none of his cows became impregnated. One day, Neil's father and his brother discussed what was wrong. As they were observing the cattle herd, the bull walked over to the scratching pole to remove insects. The bull bent his body around the scratching pole and gave himself a blow job. After the blow job, he fell to the ground and went to sleep or passed out. Neil's father laughed and said, "I think we discovered the problem." His uncle then took the bull to be slaughtered and sold for hamburger meat.

Neil thought, *I am really glad that Bill is not a bull.* He had no more contact with Bill until thirty years later when Bill called him and told him that he lived in West Hollywood and was happily married to a same-sex person. Life had been good to him, and his career had been working for a movie studio.

Neil remembered talking to a truck driver in a casino. His wife asked him, "Why were you talking to that gay man?" He hadn't noticed the gay part, but he remembered what the truck driver told him when they talked. Neil had told him that he didn't know why, but San Francisco was his favorite town in America, and he hated Los Angeles. The truck driver, who was from San Francisco, told Neil, "It's because in San Francisco we know who the queers are." Bill had accepted his label and was totally happy with it. Neil had also accepted his label as being an "expatriate oil field trash whore" who knew a thing or two about raising cows.

LABELS-TO RUSSIA WITH LOVE

T he company hired Speedy to work in the Russian Far East. He had no knowledge of the land or its people, but he was going there to work and not to socialize or study people. The Russians had discovered huge amounts of oil and gas very near Japan. The companies in Japan were hungry for the gas, but Russia had no laws allowing exports to noncommunist countries. The project had been visualized by oil companies and oil men for years, but the lack of Russian international laws and the brutal Arctic conditions had flamed out every effort to proceed with development. Russia oil companies had partnered with American and European companies on other projects, but their projects were advancing from conceptual to development at a slow pace that was full of legal and governmental agency roadblocks. The project Speedy was hired to work on was a joint venture of an American company that was partnered with a European company, but their Russian partner was the Communist Party.

The legal structure for producing oil was a maze of coordinating twenty-two state and twenty-two federal governing agencies to obtain permission to operate within the Russian law, and there were no existing Russian laws for export of oil. The proposed laws had to be written, approved, and in agreement with international laws. It seemed impossible and about as likely as America partnering with Russia to defeat Germany in WWII prior to Germany's invasion of Russia and the Japanese attacking America. Being partnered directly with the Communist Party was the only advantage the company had. Speedy knew nothing about any political party, and he remembered his grandfather telling him that if he wanted to be successful in life, he had to follow two rules: never work for the government and never owe anyone anything. Speedy had read Karl Marx's book about communism and learned some disturbing things.

Karl had been kicked out of his home country for his beliefs. His wife and children had starved to death because he was too lazy to work, and he completed his book in England only after a second-generation, very rich Britt felt guilty for being rich and wanted to share his wealth. Speedy knew that his grandfather's view on governments came from the Great Depression in the 1930s when the government decided that the price of cows was too low because there were too many cows. They came to his grandfather's ranch and shot and killed most of his cows. They then paid him the current low price for cows and buried the dead cows rather than selling the meat at market or giving it to hungry people. It made no sense, and it seemed that most government employees were lazy and didn't care about the people they were governing. Most Russians seemed to share his grandpa's thoughts.

The people on the company team were well chosen and had worked in the oil patches of the world. They fully understood that it was all about politics until you sold the first oil. The company had rented office space in the old state government office building. The office had been built during Soviet times and was the most imposing building in the city. Most of the offices were claimed and occupied according to work title or importance of the employee. Speedy's first day at work, he was assigned an office near his boss and the company lawyer. As he was given a tour of the office, he noticed two unusual things. First, it was difficult to tell the difference between Russian and American employees because most Russian employees spoke English with an American accent, and everything seemed to be well organized. Second, the bathrooms had a basket for collecting used toilet paper because the septic system could not digest the type of paper being used. It was rough and thick.

The introduction tour included going into the other employees' offices and introducing yourself. It seemed a little strange but comfortable until Speedy met the number one communist. She spoke no English, and her assistant seemed to be speaking for her, but she had large, brown, smiling eyes and seemed to know what her assistant was saying. Natasha was her name. She looked about thirty something. The large desk was hand-carved mahogany, and her chairs were the same. Everything in her office was meticulous. Speedy could not help himself when he looked into her large brown eyes. Her hair was also brown, and she seemed to observe everything about Speedy. She noticed his haircut, his Texas boots, and his belt buckle. When their eyes met, both of them felt a comfort and softness. He asked about her job, and her assistant said that she represented the Russian parties' interests, meaning she was a coordinator for all state and national agencies. Speedy smiled at her and said, "You have a difficult job." She smiled back. As they walked back to Speedy's office, the boss's secretary told Speedy that Natasha was a very important person because her father was the head of the party for the state. Speedy made a mental note to always be nice while in her presence. He felt she had understood every word he said, even if she did not speak a word of English.

The work of producing oil got hectic as each department defined a dozen reasons why they couldn't do their job. The winter got colder, and the snow got deeper. The conditions tested everyone, and some people resigned or got fired. No one got promoted, and the Russians changed their work hours from nine to five to six thirty in the morning until four in the afternoon. They had learned that most Americans began their daily work efforts early, and from around seven, it was all work. They wanted to be included and informed, so the entire team started work and finished work together. Natasha maintained the old starting and finishing times. In a few months, the brutal honesty of trying to do something that most people thought impossible cemented the team. They transformed the dozen reasons for not doing the job into two or three ways to get the job done.

By the time spring came, the team was tired, and the boss decided they needed a party. Planning a party in Russia meant simply renting a very large dance hall, buying a bottle of vodka and a case of beer for each man and a bottle of vodka and a bottle of wine for each woman, and arranging enough transportation to get all the drunks safely home. The tables had seating for ten people, and each table had two bottles of champagne. No one left the party until everything had been drank and everyone made a toast. The dance hall also had an open bar with imported whiskey. It was mandatory that each person drink and make a toast to everyone on the team. Some people drank water from vodka bottles, and these people were identified to all after the first hour because sobriety was recognized but not accepted. Their parties seem to be a ritual of seeing people shed their reservations and say what they really thought. Speedy liked the party when he remembered his grandfather's advice, "Never trust anyone that you haven't gotten drunk with."

Speedy was seated with the pipeline team and their associates. They seemed to be reminding themselves that it would be a long party, so to be slow with the drinking. Speedy was not a drinker and wasn't too interested in what the pipeliners were talking about because he had made their plan of work and already knew they would have problems with frozen terrain and mountain passes. He also knew the pipelines were intended to allow year-round production, and the first production would depend on the offshore loadings during ice-free periods. He quickly lost interest in onshore pipelines.

When a Russian girl came over and asked him to dance with her, he welcomed it. As the girl hugged him while dancing, he realized she was wearing nothing under her silk evening gown. He wanted the dance to never end, but it did. What a pleasant surprise, because he rarely saw a Russian woman who was not covered from head to toe in fur. After dancing, Speedy didn't go back to the table but went straight to the open bar and ordered American whiskey. A Britt from engineering was drinking whiskey fast, and Speedy said, "I can't believe I just danced with a woman who wasn't wearing underwear, and razor blades must be in short supply."

The Britt looked up and said, "None of them are." It seemed the silk evening gowns were easier to purchase than nonbulky women's underwear, so the women chose to not wear underwear because it messed up their lines.

After two shots of whiskey, the toasting started, and as much as he wanted to be spared, he was not. The toast was interesting, and depending on the level of sobriety, some were understandable. All toasts was translated into English or Russian. Speedy had already learned that all offices in their building were bugged, and all the good-looking women translators were KGB trained to speak English with an American accent. He learned this when one of them told Speedy that the KGB had warned them to be careful when working with Americans because America had more communists than Russia. She wanted to know if this was true. Speedy answered by saying he had no interest in politics and didn't know or care.

When it came time for Speedy to make a toast, he said, "I know our success on this job will be determined by politics. I have been a soldier who fought in a war that was determined by politics, but I am not interested in politics, and I would die before I bent down to anyone calling themselves my king or queen. I have always loved studying history because it shows how one person or a small group of people can make changes that make life better for everyone. I know for sure that my grandfathers fought with Russians to kill Germans in WWI. I know for sure that my father and my uncles fought with Russians to kill Germans in WWII. I know that my mother and aunts worked in factories, making guns to give to the Russians to kill Germans. I also know that when or if the Germans need to be killed again, there will be someone from my family and from your family willing to do the job." Most of the people were shocked to hear such a toast, especially the British. They always took exception to an American saying anything about royalty. When Speedy read the American Declaration of Independence, he often thought it could have simply said "King George, go stuff yourself." Speedy had one more shot of vodka and walked outside for the company transport to take him to his hotel. The night was cold, and the wind bit his face. He figured his brutally honest toast would surely warrant a reprimand.

The van shuttling the people drove up, and Speedy got in the back seat from the passenger's side. Natasha got in the same back seat from the driver's side at the same time. Their eyes met, and their heads touched. They sat face-to-face as the only people in the van, and a moment passed. They kissed each other, and his green eyes and her brown eyes closed. The kiss was soul rocking, as they kissed long, slowly, and passionately. They melted together as Speedy moved his hand under her dress to touch her soft breasts, and she put her hand on top, gently guiding his hand. They were lost in the moment until the door opened and her assistant laughed and said, "What are you doing? She is gay!" Speedy stopped kissing her but kept his eyes looking into her eyes and said, "Tell her that if she is gay, I want her to teach me how to be gay." Natasha smiled and started kissing him again. They stopped kissing but held hands as the vehicle received other passengers and started driving everyone home.

Natasha said something in Russian to the driver and her assistant as they drove. Her assistant said she didn't want to go home; after all the passengers were taken home, she wanted to go an after-hours club. When all the other passengers were home, only four remained: Speedy was sitting next to Natasha. Her assistant was sitting next to Natasha, and next to Speedy was his boss's assistant. It was pretty clear that on the trip to the after-hours club, they would be chaperoned by the two assistants. Three women and Speedy felt like being in a crowd, and the vodka was losing its kick.

The after-hours club was a popular place just on the outside of town, but then strangeness started happening. When they entered, the only lights on were lighting the dance floor. The club was almost full of people, but as Speedy and Natasha started dancing, people started leaving. Their chaperones were also dancing, and after a few songs of fast and furious music, Speedy left the dance floor and sat down. Natasha continued dancing as if in her own world. After some time, all the lights came on, and all the other customers were gone. Natasha continued dancing until she decided to leave. The people running the club looked relieved, but they never said a word. The club had a reputation for being a rough and tough place, but it appeared that everyone there was afraid of Natasha, except Speedy. He was a tad curious about how this beautiful lady who kissed with such grace and unbridled passion could scare everyone out of the club. And the club management had totally submitted to her wishes. He felt so safe and secure just being in her presence. Finally, her assistant told Speedy that they were going to his hotel.

They arrived at the hotel at three in the morning, and the lobby was empty. She told the assistants to wait in the lobby as she and Speedy waited for the elevator. She kissed him while the elevator took them to the fourth floor. In the room, Speedy told her he wanted a hot shower to freshen up. After he finished showering, she was sitting on the bed watching TV. She got up and went to the bath, and Speedy lay on the bed thinking about what had already happened and what was going to happen. She returned from the shower wrapped up in a large towel and lay on the bed facedown. Speedy thought she was asking herself the same questions he was asking himself, but neither spoke a single word. He wanted to explore every inch of her body, so he pulled the towel down and started kissing her back. At first, he kissed the small of her back and then continued downward, looking for hot spots. He found hot spots on her cheeks, but he continued down her legs, going up and down, kissing them from the bottom of her feet. Then he slowly kissed up her back, up her body to the top of her head. He thought it odd that the real hot spots were silver dollar–size spots on her buttocks. When he finished kissing her neck, ears, and head, she rolled over and lay on her back, looking at him. Her chocolate eyes told him how she felt, but when she closed her eyes and he kissed her eyelids, he found another hot spot. Slowly he kissed her from her eyelids down to her breasts, and the breasts seemed so soft but so firm. He kissed her down the front of her legs on both sides and finished by kissing the souls of her feet. No words were spoken, but it was her turn to kiss him, and she kissed him exactly as he had kissed her, discovering his hot spots.

The room started spinning, and they made love with each being on top and on bottom, and the rhythms were like a dance going from very slow to very fast, and the only feeling he had was being inside her and finding a response to each movement. The end eventually came as their bodies inside and out peacefully surrendered, with the only sounds coming from their fulfilled bodies. They clung to each other long after the act was over, and both knew how special this had been. Eventually, it was time for her to go home. They rode down the elevator to find the assistants and the driver sleeping in the lobby. She smiled and woke them up. She kissed Speedy one last time, and he waved goodbye as they drove away. He stood in front of the hotel in the freezing cold and thought, *I may not get fired for making the toast, but surely I will get fired for this because it was witnessed by the assistants and the driver. I could care less, because it was worth it.* Then he thought of her assistant saying, "What are you doing? She is gay." Walking up the stairs, he thought, *She sure don't deserve that label.*

They worked together for two more years but never kissed again, never spoke a word to each other except through a translator, and together they made the impossible possible. The success of the program depended on politics but not political philosophy— rather, political agencies and departments working together. Each of the twenty-two state and twenty-two federal agencies had their directives and empowerments. Speedy identified all the holdups, all the bottlenecks, and all the nonactions and how they caused program delays. Natasha identified all the requirements, all people responsible for the delays, all their concerns, and all the authorities responsible. She also identified the hierarchy for approvals and the order of presidencies for approvals. They knew exactly what the other was concerned about, and the concerns were eliminated with respect and without any confrontations.

Speedy confessed to his boss that if he wanted to fire him because of his toast at the party or for banging the daughter of the head of party, it was okay and he would understand. His boss laughed and said, "The Russians loved your toast, and from what I hear, she banged you, because some people were thinking that you both were gay because all both of you do is work, eat, and sleep."

Speedy and Natasha continued working together but in a fashion no one knew. Speedy identified the job requirements, and Natasha identified the agency requirements, and of course she made sure the agencies and departments didn't play politics with licenses, permits, and approvals. Maybe it was trust, lust, love, respect, or just a desire to do the impossible that guided them. Never was a single word spoken by either to the other without a trusted translator. They never displayed any description of the physical feelings they shared, never speaking a word about the love that they had for each other. Their work encounters had moments when they got lost looking into each other's eyes, but together they guided the program to its complete success. Success was measured by how much money the partners made, how many jobs they created, and the amount of taxes paid to the governments. The price per barrel of oil was under ten dollars when the project started, but prices changed, and the first produced oil was sold for seventy dollars per barrel. All the company and party officials were more than surprised at the economic success. After the success, many employees and party officials received honors, but Speedy and Natasha received none. Nor did they want any, and they often thought about what a coincidence it was that they were both leaving the company party at exactly the same time. They both earned the label "uncompromising workaholics."

On Speedy's last day of work, he waited outside of the office to board a bus to the airport. Suddenly, Natasha was standing by his side. She was dressed in fur, and he didn't recognize her until her chocolate eyes were looking at him. She smiled and said, "Thank you," in English as a tear rolled down her cheek. Speedy kissed her and said, "Thank you," in Russian. The other people at the bus stop watched and said nothing as Speedy got on the bus. Their tears quickly froze on their cheeks as they both looked to the sky. Frozen sparkles of rain that looked like millions of diamonds fell through the sunlight.

Three years after the project became a company, Natasha named her first son after Speedy, and Speedy named his daughter after her. The drunken toast was accurate, but the labels were not.

NEW BEGINNINGS

After boat designs and navigation systems were made definitive, ocean travel from European countries began, and European colonies started appearing in Africa, Americas, and Asia. The world became smaller, and harvesting of world resources began. Maps changed to represent the European military quest, and resources started moving from the New World to the Old World. Life changed to for 80 percent of the world's people. Most people of the New World were enslaved to harvest resources. Eventually the New World would be named the Third World after resources had been stripped and shipped to the Old World. The process continues today. In Africa and the Americas, the resources were mostly gold and silver, but in Asia, the resources were rubber and spices. Spices were most valued in the early exploitation, often more valued than gold because they enhanced life in Europe. This is a story of the Spice Islands and the enslavement of people for spices.

When the Dutch had finished exploring and conquering the area we now define as Indonesia, life for the people of Indonesia changed, as they were subjected to Dutch rule. They established laws for the populations to be those of a company, not as a government providing guarantees of freedom. They even renamed the countries, and they world named Indonesia the Dutch East Indies. The Dutch were probably the best of all colonial rulers, but their four-hundred-plus-year rule of Indonesia created a country that engulfed many smaller ancient civilizations. The driving force for colonialization was spices. The spices were mainly cloves, cinnamon, nutmeg, mace, rubber, and black pepper. The spices from Indonesia changed the world. During the fourteenth through the eighteenth centuries, spices were used for preservatives and medical treatment, and synthesized forms of these spices are still in use today. The Dutch colonized most of present-day Indonesia and ruled with full authority. They enriched themselves by trading spices that came from ancient kingdoms of different histories, religions, customs, and languages for gold and silver.

Today, Indonesia is a country made up of 16,056 named islands, and the people are a mix of the influences of spice traders from Portugal, Arabia, India, China, and most of sea-bearing Europe. The original people of Indonesia are some of the oldest in the world, dating back to 45,000 BC. Many newcomers to the country brought their own languages, religions, customs, and traditions. Thousands of years passed being governed by kingdoms before the Dutch company took total control.

Indonesia became a sovereign country after the end of World War II. Japan had controlled Indonesia during WWII because Indonesian oil fueled their war effort. Japan killed more than four million Indonesians through mass slavery and starvation. When the Japanese were defeated by America, America showed no serious interest in ruling or governing Indonesia. Only after Japan made an unconditional surrender to America did Russia and America make it perfectly clear to the world that colonies would no longer be permitted. New beginnings for many ancient counties started.

Indonesia chose their first leader. He was very smart and idealistic but naïve. He was admired by all and did his best to make his country modern and a model for living in peace. He established a common language, started an education system for all, and established the government as a three-party state. He required all people to register as a member of one of the three parties. The three parties were the parties used by most of the world at that time. They were the democratic, communist, and socialist. Indonesian people knew little about self-governance under Dutch colonial rule. Freedom was allowed, but the new government required all Indonesians to register their choice of religion and governing party. The main religions were Hindu, Buddhist, Muslim, Christian, Javanese, Subud, animism, atheism, and black magic.

The first government gave all people of Indonesian an identity, something they had lost in the long rule of colonial occupation. They were legally allowed to have family names. The new government lasted one generation before the military took control of the country, and another new beginning for Indonesia started.

The new beginnings started in 1965 when the Communist Party led an insurrection that killed most of the top military leadership in an attempt to gain full control of the power to rule. The people responded by killing more than half a million people. Most killed were those who had registered as communists. This was done in a very short time and without much response from the world. Most of the bodies were burned or tossed into the rivers. Some rivers ran red with blood for weeks, and the military went on a killing spree. The military then assumed full control of rule. The remaining communists were forbidden employment within the new government, and the party was banned. The next generation would be ruled by military but with a developing democratic form of rule that included elections and voting by all people. Cities and states developed local leadership but were closely monitored by the military. If the military decided that the opposition votes of each election indicated dissatisfaction with governing authorities, they made local leaders attend reeducation programs that made perfectly clear the government's philosophy of rule. The new military ruler was from Java, and much of the military rule had a distinct Java flavor of religion and family values that dated back to the pre-Dutch kingdoms. A most liberal form of Islam was the main religion of the time but was flavored with the ages-old religion of black magic. The island of Java contained almost half of Indonesia's population and the best educated, so the new leadership used the people of Java to provide leadership to all the other parts of the country. Java is a relatively small island, but it also contained much diversity in population, religions, and political correctness. The Javanese greatest attribute is tolerance. The identification of the people as being an Indonesian grew stronger, but their tolerant nature forced the third generation to make another new beginning.

The leadership decided to repopulate the remaining 16,055 islands with people from Java, and the great Indonesia transmigration began. The transmigration consisted mostly of the least desirable or politically incorrect populous of Java, but the opportunity for them to own land was also a motivator, as it elevated their independence. The lands given to them would be mostly in the jungles and rain forests, where traditional farming would be difficult, but with guidance from the government's agriculture people, they learned what survival crops and cash crops would grow there. They also learned what the jungles would provide for free and the importance of coexistence. Many would leave their new beginnings and find their way back to Java, but some would have success and tame the jungles and rain forests by burning them, using the ashes to plant crops to survive. Some would be eaten by tigers, trampled by elephants, or eaten by snakes, but they learned from the indigenous people how to survive, and they blended in with the native indigenous people as much as the native people blended in with them.

Long before the government transmigration program started, the Javanese were moving to the other islands in pursuit of employment. They blended into the other cultures because they all identified as being Indonesian, and they all spoke the same language. The new beginnings were a success, and the people of Indonesia learned how important having a family name really is. They spread the importance of self-dependence, ownership, education, and family history. The third generation would lead Indonesia in becoming the ninth largest producer of oil and gas and creating an economy with the nineteenth largest gross domestic product numbers.

The third generation of government was called a guided democracy, and they had already learned lessons in absolute power, disrespect, and greed. They would also learn that the comfort of a new house with amenities would never equal the comfort of sleeping in a rain forest in a thatched hut made from the jungle leaves, trusting God to protect them, and the smell and comfort of fresh rain that enabled their dreams of living for tomorrow without regrets from today.

For ten years, I lived and worked in Indonesia. I slept in their jungles and rain forest. I slept in their resorts and their five-star hotels in Jakarta. I worked with the educated people in Jakarta and the indigenous people from many named and unnamed islands. I never noticed a difference in character because they are all Indonesians of the same heart and mind. New beginnings for the hundred million people worked because they never forgot their past.

ALBERT RAY, THE BRAVEST MAN I EVER KNEW

Al and Albert Ray were in the same class during elementary school. They shared the same school bus seat for five years. They became friends and talked during the hour ride to and from school. In their classes, they were the only boys. The nine girls in the class didn't seem interested in having anything to do with either of them and rarely talked to them. During lunch and recess, they hung out with other kids in other grades because they were monitored by their brothers and sisters as well as the teachers. In their earlier grades, they had always joined each other on the playground swings. But then Albert Ray convinced Al that if they moved the playground swing fast enough and high enough, eventually the swing would make a loop, and they would be the first in school to make a loop on the school swings. So each day, they would make the swings go as fast and as high as they could. The day came when Al went too high, and the swing stalled and fell straight down; he held on for dear life as the fall from fifteen feet high broke the swing seat and one of the chains holding the seat. The teachers got involved and questioned their sanity and mentioned something called physics, which neither Al nor Albert Ray understood or believed. To them, looping a swing was as simple as tying a rock on a string, holding the string in their hand, and then swinging the rock until it looped around their finger. They abandoned the swings and seesaws to play in the creek behind the school—until the day they were building a dam across the creek.

They worked with abandon to dam up the creek and save the school from flooding. Several other boys joined them until the school bell rang, telling everyone to go back to class. Albert Ray told Al that he would go talk to the teacher and tell them that building the dam was more important than class and ask the teacher if they could continue working. Al continued his dam work, and Albert Ray came back and said that the teacher said it was okay to continue. They continued to pile sticks in the creek and cover them with dirt. All was well for twenty minutes, and then the school principal arrived to inform them that they had to return to class—but not before they went with him to his office for three paddle swats on their backsides. The paddling was the first for Al, and his butt didn't hurt nearly as much as his pride when the others in class smiled at him. He never again trusted Albert Ray, but they remained friends until Al cheated him out of his twenty-five cents lunch money.

They both collected pennies, and each day on the school bus, when they had a new penny, they would show it as the newest member of their collection and talk about what pennies they needed for their collection. One day they talked about the 1943 pennies, as 1943 was the year they were born. The 1943 pennies were made out of tin because the usual copper was required to manufacture war supplies during WWII. Albert Ray said that 1943 was the only year pennies were made from zinc, and Al got an idea. The idea was to use the mercury from his grandpa's thermometer to coat a copper penny. Al loved playing with mercury because it reacted to movement and magnets in such a funny way. If you dropped a spot of mercury, you could use a magnet to move the little dots into the original shape. You could also push and pull mercury with a magnet, being careful not to allow the mercury to attach to the magnet. Al thought he could electroplate the penny if he could use a battery, but the idea never worked. He then took a small spot of mercury and used his thumb and finger to rub the mercury into the copper penny. It worked, so he used mercury to coat pennies of different dates. He used a moist linen cloth to polish the mercury-coated penny. Al was in the fourth grade, so he had not learned all the dangers of mercury, and neither had most people, because nonmercury thermometers were not in common use. Al also learned that you could use mercury to complete an electrical connection. The electrical connections were DC because neither Albert's nor Al's homes had AC electricity.

On the school bus, Al ask Albert Ray if he was sure that 1943 was the only year that pennies were made of zinc. He answered yes, he was sure. Al took the mercury-coated penny dated 1945 and showed it to him. Al said, "I have this really rare penny," and Albert Ray wanted it. After some bargaining, he traded it for the quarter Albert Ray had for his lunch money. A few days later, after the mercury had regrouped, he realized he had been cheated out of his lunch money. They remained friends, but he would never trust Al again.

Al had watched Albert Ray struggle with learning disabilities from the first grade, when he was punished for not remembering his ABCs, up until sixth grade, where he struggled with homework. Al never accepted or understood his learning disabilities and never considered that he was smarter or dumber than Albert Ray, but he often thought about Albert Ray's problem of having an alcoholic father and a mother who was overly religious. He knew Albert Ray had at least a dozen brothers and sisters who did just fine in school, and one of his brothers worked for a bank and had gone to college. Albert Ray dropped out of school during eighth grade, a year before high school started. His parents said that he was no longer interested in school. Al was shocked and hurt because he became the only boy in his class. He also felt so sad when the school bus would stop to pick up his brothers and sisters, and Al would see Albert Ray in the field, plowing the crops with a plow pulled by a mule.

Mules are a hybrid between a horse and a donkey, but they have attitudes and personalities different from horses or donkeys. Mules can work hard all day, and they need little training. Before the availability of heavy equipment, the men cutting logs from the national forest had mules they would hook to a log. The mules would find a way to pull the large logs through the forest, back to their feeding and watering pens. Texans had pride in owning a Missouri mule. During the Depression years, all small farms produced both self-sustaining food crops and cash crops with mules. Albert Ray and his mule assumed this role for his family. It made Al shocked and sad to see this happen to his friend.

School became a place for Al to hide in reading books and learning from teachers. He rarely talked to anyone on the school bus. When challenged, he would fight, but the older boys quickly learned that Al would not only fight them, he never fought fair, and he would fight them every day, so they usually left him alone. Al thought it strange that the girls were paying him more attention, especially when he was required to write a story or a poem that his teacher read to the class. To see their stares turning into soft eyes of compassion meant nothing to him.

When Albert Ray's father was drinking, he would sit alone on his front porch, but if he was sober, his wife and family would join him. Al's father would sometimes stop and visit if he wasn't drinking. When they stopped by to visit, Al usually stayed near the truck because Albert Ray's brothers and sisters thought Al was crazy because of an incident that had happened a few years earlier. They all attended a radical Pentecostal church, and most folks named them the "Bench Jumpers" because in church services they would get in the spirit and jump benches and talk in different languages. Al didn't think their church strange, because his uncle's church taught that everyone was going to hell except them. Mostly, Al remembered their sermons about going to hell for watching television. Al and his brothers farmed cotton for a season so they could buy a TV. Their father told them that if the really wanted a TV, they had to earn it. They earned it at their ages of twelve, ten, and eight years old when they raised, picked, and sold their first bale of cotton. A few months later, the same church members came to visit. They sat in their family living room watching the Grand Old Opry live from Nashville on the boys' hard-earned TV. Al and his brothers learned the word *hypocrite* and would never forget it.

None of the Pentecostals watched TV in their living room, but they would get twenty-five or thirty members of their church sitting and standing on the bed of a pulpwood-hauling truck to stop in front of their house to sing religious songs. One day, they stayed too long, and the boy's mother waved for them to move on. They ignored her, so Al took out the 12-gauge shotgun and fired a shot in their direction. He aimed well behind them, but when the small-size squirrel shots hit the dusty road, they quickly drove on. Al thought no one could say he was trying to shoot and kill them because it was more than one hundred yards from the house and he had to elevate the shotgun forty-plus degrees just to hit the road. His defense may not have held up in court, but they never came back trying to convert Al's family to their bench jumping. When questioned, Al told his father that he had seen a mad dog trying to attack the singers. Al's father had to talk to the local judge about the incident, but the point was made—no more shooting while people were driving down the road. Al thought that if the boys had to mind their mother, so did everyone. Al felt bad because Albert Ray's mother and sisters were on back of that truck.

If they stopped by to visit Albert Ray's family, the boys and Albert Ray's brothers would meet and talk in their barn. One day when they stopped by to visit, Albert Ray was talking about how mean the mule was. The mule worked just fine, but when he was hooking her up to a bridle, pulling the collar and harness to pull the turning plow for starting work, the mule would kick and try to bite him. Albert said he was going to screw the mule to teach her a lesson. All the boys gathered at the corral to watch. He hooked her to the harness, and the action started when he stood his 4'5" body on wood boards halfway up the side of the corral and made the mule back up to him. He held the reins so the mule backed up straight to him. The mule started kicking and trying to turn her head to bite him, but he dodged each kick. The corral wood boards started breaking as the mule landed kicks near Albert Ray. The battle with the mule lasted a few minutes; she destroyed the corral fence, but her kicks never hit him. No sex was performed, but when it ended, the mule was gentler, probably because the bit in her jaw pulled blood because of Albert Ray pulling back hard on the reins. The lesson stopped when his father yelled from the front porch for them to get out of the corral and quit playing with the mule.

Albert Ray would never return to riding the school bus, but each morning as the school bus stopped by their house to pick up his brothers and sisters, Al would see him hooking up the mule, getting ready for a day's work plowing in the fields. What kind of learning disability he had would never be known, but most likely it was a vision problem. Certainly it was not a physical or mental problem. All Al could think of was the day in school while they were in the sixth grade and the teacher made them write a poem. Albert Ray didn't write a poem; he wrote a song and sang it for the class. The name of the song was "Don't Sell Daddy Any More Whiskey." In the song, he had verses about how his father changed when he drank whiskey. The first time Al heard him sing the song, he thought about his own grandfather making and selling whiskey. He would always remember Albert Ray as being the bravest fourteen-year-old man he had ever known.

Albert Ray would continue working on the family farm until he passed away. He would never have another job but would replace the mule with heavy construction equipment and would master each piece of the equipment to maximize its use in moving dirt and rocks. He would never be in the military serving his country because he could not read or write, and he had fathered three children before his twenty-first birthday. After his death, his older brother married his widow and became father to his children. He would never be a preacher, but he would remain religious and would never drink whiskey. After his father passed away, he would assume the role of head of his family, even though he had older brothers and sisters. When the day came that his tractor flipped over backward and crushed him to death, he would be remembered for who he was and the people he helped. Al would always remember him as being the youngest and bravest man he had ever known.

TIGERS OF SUMATRA

The tigers of Sumatra often eat people. When a person is killed by a tiger, the military hunts down the tiger and kills it, and life goes on. The military examines the dead tigers for having gold teeth. If gold teeth are found, they know the tiger is a not normal tiger who eats wild pigs and monkeys; the tiger is the reincarnation of some rich person who must continue to live for their sins as a man-eating tiger. Normally the tiger kills the person by biting the neck and using its back legs to rip out the vital organs. It always eats the liver and lungs first, then the person's thighs. The people don't have guns, and people are easier to catch than wild pigs or monkeys, but only man-eaters eat people. Most man-eaters are old and slow tigers who can no longer catch wild pigs and monkeys, but it's not uncommon for the police to find a gold tooth.

Elephants, tigers, and even rhinos can be found in Sumatra. They also have man-eating snakes, but what Neil learned from working for seven years in Central Sumatra is that the Sumatra people are the most interesting. Central Sumatra was blessed with oil—black gold, Texas tea. Oil brought war when the Japanese needed oil to run their war machine. After the war, an American oil company ran the oil field as partners with the Indonesian government, and 95 percent of the forty thousand employees were Indonesian citizens. Some of the Americans had been banished to a foreign assignment, but most were specialized engineers, geologists, or managers of some sort. At peak production, the oil fields produced more than one million barrels per day. The oil field workers come from all over Indonesia and all over the world.

Neil worked in the exploration group. His job was to build roads and bridges to the new drilling sites and to build power lines and pipelines from the new wells. The first time he saw a corduroy road being built through the jungle, he was both disturbed and amazed. Corduroy roads were built by cutting down the forest and placing the logs as a base for the road, because under the jungles were mostly swamps. Once the logs were aligned, they were covered with compacted sand, and the roads allowed the movement of heavy equipment and a drilling rig. When the construction supervisor asked what Neil thought of their roads, he said, "I think that in the future some will be mining the roads for all the teak and mahogany logs, because in the future, those logs will be worth a fortune." The construction manager looked at him as if he thought Neil worked for Green Peace and was trying to save the forest. He wasn't trying to save the forest; he was trying to find oil and improve lives.

He had seen primitive people living deep in the jungles, and the first time he saw them, he was shocked that they were naked. When the construction crews appeared, the people shot at the crews with their bows and spears until one of the construction supervisors gave them some clothes. Once they put on clothes, they stopped shooting and started working for the company. It seemed that their small clearings and fire were their only security from the jungle, which was full of predators. Their stomach skin was baggy from over and undereating, but they were healthy people. After becoming employees, they became good workers.

The company and its contractors employed more than forty thousand employees and dependents. The company built five cities to house their people. The cities included schools, hospitals, and recreation facilities. The expatriates came from many countries, and the Indonesians came from all parts of Indonesia. Outside the company towns, local villages appeared that provided for the contractors who weren't given housing in the company towns. Production pipelines had service roads and power line right of ways. These roads opened up the jungles to the farmers and timber crews. When the oil field expanded, the jungles became farms and palm oil plantations because all the neighboring countries had big appetites for sugar, paper, and wood. Harvesting trees was illegal, but no one observed the laws. Slowly the jungles were cleared, and the tigers slowly disappeared.

The province in central Sumatra was named Riau, and oil seemed to be all over the entire area. As the oilfields grew, Indonesians from all of Indonesia flocked to Riau to work. The company provided good housing, a commissary, schools, and a retirement plan.

Neil quickly learned to identify the ethnic diversity of the Indonesian people.

The task of collecting data from work efforts and identifying manpower and equipment requirements for future work needed improvement. The collection of data was done manually because no computers were available, and the male clerks were very low-paying positions. The company's first response to fill this need was to hire and train women. Jobs for women were few because they only worked in human resources. Neil was made to start a training program for the newly hired women but had no say in their qualifications. It was a sort of punishment because he had demanded something be done to improve the data being used to plan work. All the women hired were relatives of employees. Surprisingly, most of them were well educated and spoke English, but their hiring did present problems because the men found every excuse in the book to talk to and flirt with them. The women's personalities soon became apparent, and the men learned which ones to flirt with and to never come into their office to flirt with them. The leadership among the women became apparent, and they became protective of one another. They were all pioneers because previously the company didn't hire women. As they decorated their cubicles and offices, it added a woman's touch.

Al had reservations about hiring women, but after witnessing an incident, he decided he was wrong. A lady name Helmi was a natural leader, and she usually spoke for the other women. She was a Batak from the Lake Toba region. This is a region that the Dutch missionaries had managed to Christianize, but they were a robust tribe, and their neighbors were mostly a very radical Islamic colony that was feared. The Batak managed to remain Christian, but their reputation for being cannibals remained, particularly for eating Dutch.

Helmi was a born leader but shy about women working with men. The day came when an employee was killed in an accident, and their expatriate boss told them to prepare for a company funeral. This consisted of paying the family blood money (usually a year's pay) and expressing sympathy to the family. Helmi decided to make wreaths of flowers to give to the family, but there was no florist. She requested that Al and Jose go with her to pick flowers. Al drove around looking for flowers, and Helmi gathered flowers and tree blooms.

Orchids grew wild, but in the camp, most were in someone's yard. Al told her to take the flowers from where she found them, but the tree blooms that she wanted were next to the welding fabrication shop. She picked the blooms until some of the men stopped work and made catcalls at her. They also said, "Nice ass, good boobs." Jose told her let us look elsewhere. Helmi smiled at them and thanked the men for their compliments, then told them that she was picking flowers for the funeral of an employee who had been killed in an accident. Something amazing happened. All the men stopped working, asked her which blooms she wanted, and started climbing the trees to get them. Al was sure the expatriate boss would be upset because of the work stoppage, but he didn't care. The thirty-plus men quickly gathered the flowers and expressed their thanks to her. She smiled the same smile as when they told her she had a nice ass and good boobs. The expat shop foreman was not upset, but the wife of the employee who provided the orchids was. Helmi and Al were reported as orchid thieves. Al showed his East Texas temper by saying, "So what?" Helmi gave Al that same smile she had given the workers while gathering flowers.

The offices smelled better because of their daily flowers, the offices were cleaner, and the spoken language was softer and more direct. They enjoyed compiling statistics and metrics of ongoing work. Soon they produced more data than their bosses could digest. Al decided they all needed computers so that data could be managed, merged, and used to save money. Oil prices were very low, and cost had to be controlled. The company would not buy computers, so Al went to Singapore, bought two computers, and started training the women. The data was collected in databases, spreadsheets were made, and graphics were produced to show manpower and equipment requirements so that 2,500 men and 750 pieces of heavy equipment could be managed. The company noticed, and the bosses were impressed, so they agreed to pay Al for the use of his computers. The oil company also noticed, and they started buying computers. Most of the computers were Compaq knockoffs, but DOS was a common operating system, and Al had been trained in computer operation systems. Very quickly, each employee had a name and work skill, and this drove a training program. Each piece of equipment was identified, and a classification for use was established.

This allowed planned maintenance and better job planning. As the women started cranking out work plans, the flirting seemed to stop, and the oil company was impressed with the cost of work reductions, so they asked Al to set up a training program and ordered more/better computers. Helmi set the rules for working women. She was a Sumatra tiger.

After the training program became routine, Al spent more and more time in the field, watching the execution of the work. He knew that the craft supervision by other expatriates was not sufficient and that poor workmanship equaled higher cost. Most expatriates were afraid to go into the jungle. Sumatra roads were dangerous, and the rains were blinding because most of East Sumatra was either a coastal swamp or a rain forest, and most of the expatriates were lazy. Most of the expats were former American contractors who had worked in Vietnam and married Vietnamese wives. They were afraid to go home; many had tried, but their own families would not accept them. Al remembered them as the big-money guys in Vietnam who got paid too much and partied too much in war, and he didn't like or trust them.

Once a week, all the staff went to a meeting where each manager was questioned about their weekly work. In one of these meetings, Al was sitting across from an Australian Vietnam vet and next to an American vet. At the other end of the table sat the Vietnam contractors. Before the meeting started, everyone was quiet except the Vietnam contractors. One of them said, "I can't believe I worked in Vietnam all those years, and I never made more than $2,500 per month. Plus we got shot at."

Al looked at the Aussie vet and the American vet and said, "I only made $235 per month, but I got to shoot back, and if I was lucky, I got to shoot first." They both laughed so hard the meeting started immediately.

Jose was a Pilipino by birth but had been working in Sumatra for many years. He would always be remembered as Al's best friend. He came to Sumatra when his mother sent him to work with and be supervised by his father. Jose had gotten into some serious trouble in Manila. Jose's family was strongly Catholic, and his father had worked with Americans during WWII, but Jose was like no one else. He was just Jose. Al and Jose became such good friends that their coworkers called them Hose A and Hose B. Jose was like a brother to Al. No comment was too stupid, no idea was too bad, and they never had a bad word to say to each other. They shared many great times together, some sad times, and all family secrets. They ate breakfast, lunch, and supper together every day for three years. They drove through jungles together every day, and there was never a single difference in beliefs, likes, or dislikes. When Al got distracted, Jose noticed, and when Jose was troubled, Al noticed. They trusted each other with their lives.

While driving through the jungles, Al would see wild animals. Bears, tigers, cougars, elephants, and man-eating snakes were seen with a regularity that frightened Jose. On the day they saw a cobra-like snake that was bigger than a light pole and more than twenty feet long, Jose freaked out because Al tried to run over it. Al wanted the skin of the snake to make a new pair of cowboy boots. The snake was too smart and stood up on his tail. Al went around him and then started backing up the truck to run over the snake. The snake, standing up on his tail, seemed to be looking down on them. It had a four-foot-wide hood like a cobra's, but the most unusual part was his color—purple with yellow trimming. The exhaust fumes from the vehicle caused the snake to lie down and move into the jungle. Jose was livid about Al trying to run over the snake. Al asked Jose what kind of a snake they had seen. Jose said that the snake used to be an evil Chinese person who was sent back to life as a snake to pay for his sins. Al told him that he had never read about or heard about such a snake, so maybe he was right. When they returned to the camp, Al told the other workers about what they had seen. When he said the snake was bigger than a light pole, had a cobra hood, stood on his tail, was at least three feet in diameter, and was purple and yellow, everyone laughed and suggested they didn't need to drink or smoke on the job. They asked Jose how big the snake was, and he opened his hand to the size of a softball. They again laughed as Al and Jose left.

Outside the club, Al ask Jose, "Why did you tell a lie? You saw the snake."

Jose said, "I have never trusted white guys except you, and they didn't believe you, so I just made them feel better. They are already afraid of going into the jungle, but somehow the damn animals want to show themselves to you, and I really don't understand it."

Al told Jose that animals only show themselves to people they trust.

Months later, Al was aboard a plane bound for Amsterdam, sitting next to a Dutchman who had unusual tattoos on his arms. He explained that he worked in Indonesia catching animals for Zoos in Europe and America. His tattoos were given by tribes granting him permission to travel in their territories. Al told him about the mysterious snake, and the man got excited and told Al he had only heard of the snake, but it was famous among the tribe's people, and he would pay $10,000 for the snake—dead or alive.

Several years later, a friend from Australia told Al he had the skin of a snake like the one Al had described, and he would trade it for one of the diamonds that Al found while working in Saudi Arabia. They agreed, and when the swap was made, the skin was the right snake but only about seven feet long. His friend explained that skin came from a nest of baby snakes, not a full-grown adult.

Jose was a tiger of Sumatra and spent most of his life watching as palm oil plantations and timber companies slowly destroyed the rain forest by using the same roads they had built to open up the jungle.

Maybe the animals who showed themselves to Al and Jose were crying for help, and they didn't know it.

After computers defined the metrics for the use of 750 pieces of heavy equipment used in maintenance and new construction, a study was made to identify fuel use. The study revealed that fuel theft was a major problem, and more fuel was stolen than was being used. The Vietnam contractors were determined to control and stop the stealing. They made some effort, but their fear of going into the jungle where the equipment was being used prevented any success. They decided to put a color dye into all the fuel, installed meters to monitor hours of use, and made each operator sign for the amount of fuel put into equipment tanks, but they couldn't stop the theft. Al and Jose spent more time in the jungle than all of the Vietnam contractors together, but neither had any interest in fuel theft and watched as efforts to stop it failed. They set up checkpoints along the main roads to check for stolen fuel but caught no one. Al thought employees were stealing it for personal use, but few employees had vehicles. Jose thought they were selling it to the few gas stations who were all government owned. Neither Al nor Jose cared about employees stealing fuel.

The most southern part of the oil field was in a saltwater tidal swamp, a horrible place to work because the swamp water rose and sank with the tides of the Malacca Strait. Everyone who worked there was afraid of salt water because of the saltwater crocodiles. A very large river ran to the ocean and flooded the area with fresh water. Then the ocean would bring in high tides, and the same area would be flooded with salt water. This area was identified as the center of the fuel theft problem, but no one had ever caught even a single thief. Crocodiles and man-eating fish filled the brackish water, and few Indonesians liked to venture into the swamps filled with man-eaters.

Most of the produced oil was fed to feeder lines flowing into the main pipeline going to a port and a refinery, but one small pipeline ran in the opposite direction to a small port. The pipeline metering system identified the pipeline either had a leak or someone was stealing the oil. Jose and Al were sent to investigate. They arranged for a boat ride down the mighty Siak River. The Siak River is almost the same as the as the Missouri River because it starts from the mountains and runs through the jungles and swamps to the ocean. The riverbanks are covered with foliage. The crew accompanying Jose and Al included a government-relations employee, and he was carrying a large handbag. No questions were asked as they enjoyed the three-hour boat ride down the river to the spot of the leak.

Upon arrival, they quickly found a spot in the top of the oil pipeline with a neatly drilled hole. Around the pipeline was a pool of crude oil. As they inspected the surroundings, Al saw a fisherman building a large fishing boat. He fashioned the sides of the boat with dried lumber layered with overlays of smaller boards. The hull was amazingly accurate in height, shape, and width and was being built one board at a time. A small fire was burning near the boat, and Al observed the man was adding crude oil to the boat hull. As he coated the boards with crude oil, he would take a burning palm leaf and set the oil on fire to seal the boat's seams. As the flames burned, he would quickly put out the fire and pour water on the seams. Al realized he was waterproofing the boat, and the man paid no attention to Al or the crew. Jose and Al laughed and said, "I think all we need to fix the pipeline is a cork for the drilled hole." The pipeline was not pressurized, and only when the company pumped oil on board the small tankers did the oil reach the top of the pipeline. There was no theft to report, and instead of a cork, they would install a valve so the boat makers could get their required crude oil and contain it in the small pond. No harm, no foul. It was just fishermen making a living.

After the leak had been resolved and a valve placed in the drilled hole, it was almost lunchtime, but there would be no lunch until after a four-hour boat ride back up the river. Al noticed a small village about half a mile down the river and told Jose that he was walking down to see if they had any food and drink for sale. Al was thirsty in the hundred-degree weather and 99 percent humidity. Jose said, "Please don't go there. The crew said it was too dangerous." Al was surprised because it looked so peaceful. He ignored Jose and started walking toward the village. Jose followed him but a few yards behind, and neither the crew nor the government man followed.

Al walked into the village and saw only a small restaurant and one waitress. He walked in, sat down, and asked for a Coke with ice. The waitress, who spoke perfect English, brought him a Coke with ice. He looked at the buffet-style food as Jose joined him but said nothing. Al had the waitress identify all the food to him, and he ordered. As Jose and Al ate, the crew and government man showed up and joined them. Al noticed the waitress was Chinese, and after the crew started eating, other men and women from the village entered the open-air restaurant. Al paid no attention to the Chinese talk or the Indonesian talk, but he did notice how white skinned the Chinese were. He thought it odd that they were so fair skinned in spite of living near the equator. After eating, the government man opened his handbag and paid for everything. Al and Jose were too busy looking at the waitresses to feel any presence of animosity.

They got on the boat and went back up the river. Al felt like something was missing, and it was. He would learn that that small village across the straits from Singapore was a dangerous place because it was accessible only by water and the pipeline right of way, and the pipeline road had twenty-four-hour guards to alert the villagers to leave. In 1965, Indonesians went on a killing spree because of an attempted coup, and the killing spree included Chinese. Thirty years later, no one trusted anyone, and the government man had been carrying a bag of money as a safety weapon.

Al and Jose had been set up by the Vietnam lazy-ass cowards because they knew the story.

Al and Jose had made some new friends, and one of the crew had been closely watching Al and Jose. Al invited him to stop by his office and visit him. Sap was a tiny man who looked neither Indonesian nor Chinese. He was less than five feet tall and didn't weigh a hundred pounds, but he had beautifully intelligent, smiling eyes and an easy laugh. He kept his promise to Al of coming by his office for a visit. He waited for Al to return from a meeting and started playing with Al's computer. Al came in, and Sap was embarrassed at being caught. Al looked at the computer screen and quickly told Sap to keep playing so he could see what he knew. Al noticed that Sap was not looking at the computer programs; he was looking at the BIOS programming. No one except Al knew what the BIOS was. Al had studied system programming, and Sap had never lived outside the jungle. Sap explained that he had never touched a computer, but he had read many books about computers. Al questioned him about his ethnic bloodlines, and he said his family members were the original people to the area, and most of his family had been killed by Japanese in WWII. Al told him that he wanted to hire him, and Sap was excited. Al explained that he didn't know about the dangers of the pipeline inquiry because his wig-wearing boss hadn't told him. Sap said, "You showed no fear. I personally know some of those Chinese people, and they are good people who have been in Indonesia for a very long time."

Al told his wig-wearing Vietnam contractor boss that he wanted to hire Sap, but his boss said, "No way, because he is involved with the fuel theft." Al went over his head to the next boss, where he also explained how his boss had not told him about the dangers of going to the Chinese village. He had also learned that the Indonesian Army could not go there and how that village was where all the smuggled-in duty-free things from Singapore went. He demanded that he transfer Sap to him. The big boss agreed, and the Vietnam contractors were pissed at Al. He couldn't care less and spent more time in the jungle.

Jose was teaching him about Muslim Indonesians, and Al was teaching Jose about the jungle animals, and they became brothers. Al went to see Sap to tell him that he would be working in Al's office and to tell him about the fuel stealing. Sap was happy and explained how much he loved being in the jungle, but he had fallen in love and planned to get married, and even though the village chief had given him land, he still had to build a house. He explained how he was spending his two-dollars-per-day wages and how he stole fuel only to buy lumber to build his house. Al told him he would now make five dollars a day, but he couldn't keep stealing fuel. Sap was so happy he hugged Al. Al asked him how much fuel he was stealing, and Sap told him it was two liters per week, just enough to buy two boards per week.

Al left Indonesia and didn't get to see Sap develop. When Al returned to Indonesia ten years later, he learned that Sap had become a government environmental coordinator for the oil company and a consultant for the government. He not only built his house; he was raising five children. Al went to see him, and Sap was so surprised he jumped from his desk and hugged Al's neck like a small child. When someone smiled at seeing Mr. Professional hugging a foreigner, he was quickly and quietly told to go outside, that this was private. The smiles turned to tears as they talked. Sap was the real Sumatran tiger and would spend his life protecting them.

CARLOS

Carlos & Making a Living

Al was tired of being a soldier and he was tired of seeing people and places destroyed. The Viet Nam war seemed to have no end in sight. After 1968 most of the communist armies had already been destroyed and the war was being directed by politics. He began to understand what his brother Joe had told him in 1966, after Joe had completed his second tour of duty in Viet Nam; he said "Killing people is just too easy." "It should be harder than killing animals for food but it's not, it's just too easy." When his brother told him this he knew his brother was telling the truth but he thought "Yes it too easy for you because you have a helicopter gunship strapped to your ass and you can see like an Eagle and run like a Deer" but Al could always tell when his brother was lying and he knew that his brother was telling the truth.

Six month later he learned how true his brother's words were because finding the enemy and killing the enemy was too easy. Any time the enemy moved they could be seen by the spies in the skies and all it took to kill them was a phone call to the bombers. The push of a button and the enemy got killed. If the bombers were grounded or busy, the helicopters or the gunships could kill them; if they were busy a team of soldiers could kill them. Killing was just too easy and the politicians tried to make it harder by defining the boundaries of war and giving the enemy a safe haven where American could not use its killing machines. The enemy took advantage by using the geographic safe havens to stock pile weapons and troops and every day Al could look at maps showing where the enemy was and what they were planning from their safe havens that was being provided by the demanding politicians and that the war must be fought within the geographic boundaries of the countries involved. The safe havens in Laos and Cambodia became homes for the enemy and the might Mekong River a natural boundary. The war was no longer interesting as the politicians decided no one should win. Al lost interest in the war while he was looking thru the belongings of recently kill North Viet Nam Officer and all he found of importance was a photograph of the officer, his wife and small son. They were all smiling as if happier times were just around the bend instead of him being buried in a shallow grave in the jungle in another country where no one would ever know. It all seemed so very wrong and yet Al could not figure out exactly what was wrong, but he thought "Yes killing people is too easy."

Al requested the Army to give him an early separation so he could attend college and the Army agreed. He felt bad leaving his team but they would soon follow him to life outside the military. The war was over on the 4th of July 1970. He would still remain in the army reserves for another 2 years but he knew that would be a non-event because America had lost its stomach for war and yes "killing was too easy."

The airplane ride to Oakland, California was uneventful after departure but during departure they were told that only one 68 pound duffle bag could be checked as baggage. One soldier had packed his 68 pound duffle bag completely full of marijuana. He wasn't arrested but the bag of drugs was taken by the Air force. None of the members of Al's team used drugs but he had seen and heard about how drugs had been given to soldiers for free. The war was over but when Al asks the soldier who lost his bag "What do you think will happen when the drug users get home?" The soldier laughed and started singing a WWII song "After the boys have been to Paris, you can't keep them down on the farm." Everyone laughed.

The stay in Oakland was short and busy. Their job was to process you out of the Army and they had lots of experience so things went fast. The same day they arrived they were fed well, paid in full, given a new uniform and bussed to San Francisco for a flight home. It was on the bus ride that he was seated by and talked to a kid from New Orleans. He had received a Dis Honorable discharge and he received no pay and was going to hitch hike a ride home. He told Al his leader didn't like him and his new leader had gotten innocent soldiers killed. He had done two tours in Nam and the scars on his fore arms told and showed what he did. He was in field artillery and the burn marks came from loading a hot 105 artillery gun. He had been a good soldier until he got a leader who got his friends killed. Al had been paid for the 3 months of leave he had never taken so he bought the soldier an airplane ticket. The flight would go to Las Vegas, then to Houston and on to New Orleans. When they boarded they sat at window seats on opposite sides of the plane. From San Francisco to Vegas the plane was about half full and no one drank or talked. When the flight left from Vegas it was full. Next to Al was a large man who spoke in Italian and smelled of whiskey and garlic. Al had been reading a newspaper looking for ideas about making a living. He could never go back to his previous line of work because the last mortar attach and injured him and the pain was constant. He needed to learn fast and when the bad smelling man reached up and turned his reading light off he felt a surge of bad news. He turned the light back on while looking the man in the eye. The man saw something in Al's eyes that told him "don't go there". On the aisle seat was a short man who witnessed the entire happening. He smiled and nodded at Al. Everyone on board seemed to be sleeping except Al and the two men in the aisle seats who were talking and listening. Al listened to their conversation and quickly lost interest because they were discussing business and financing projects. Al noticed that the short man was giving his blessings to the skinny man who was dressed in a Neman Marcos top dollar suit. The deals were defined by the skinny man and the short man was giving his approval.

The airplane could not land at the Houston airport because of the fog, the pilot told them they would go on to New Orleans and then return to Houston. When the landed at New Orleans they were all sent to a holding gate and were told that even the New Orleans bound passengers could not depart. They must re-board the flight back to Houston then return to New Orleans. It seemed crazy but an airline employee explained that no one could leave the gate because it was considered an unplanned landing. All New Orleans passengers must fly back to Houston and then return to New Orleans. Rules were rules and no one seemed to mind. As they waited at the holding gate Al and his new friend the dishonorable discharged soldier started conversation about how they would find work outside the Army. They were unaware where the after the army road would take them, they had no plans and didn't know what kind of work was available but they talked. Al planned to go back to college and finish his degree but he needed a job to pay bills. The New Orleans soldier talked about working with the Long Shore men or a security company. The security job sounded interesting and neither of them knew anything about rate of pay or job requirements. As they talked Al noticed that the short man from the flight was listening to them. Al sensed that the New Orleans soldier already knew the short man because and when the short man engaged them in conversation; the soldier was very quiet and respectful. The short man thanked them for their service in the Army and told them that if they couldn't find work to contact him. He handed them a business card and told them they could find him by showing the card to anyone in New Orleans. It seemed odd that everyone in New Orleans would know him but his care and interest in the soldiers seemed very real. Al didn't read the card and simply put it in his shirt pocket. The other soldier told him "Thank you very much and I will come to see you." After the conversation the short man walked away to talk to the skinny man and Al looked at the card. The card was blank on the back and on the front side it read only "Carlos." Al thought it so strange that everyone in New Orleans would know Carlos and Al would keep the card in his wallet for the next 10 years. During the 10 years he would learn in detail exactly who Carlos was and there were many times he wanted to go see Carlos but he never went to see him.

Al found a job but it was more like a job finding him. The large chemical company was hiring and they were hiring only Viet Nam veterans. Al was hired and initially worked in a chemical plant. He worked there for a short time until they noticed his security clearance. Al had the highest security clearance the US government allowed. Someone in corporate noticed and it was someone who had served in the same outfit that Al served in. He knew that Al was someone who could keep a secret. Al was told he must complete college and if he agreed they would waive the college degree requirement. He was already enrolled so agreed and started his coat and tie job. The coat and tie job requirements were simple but a little strange that required that if he left his office to go to the bathroom, he must wear his coat and he must wear a tie to enter the building.

His new boss must review all plans for spending company money. All economic packages required approval by the company's board of directors. All economic packages must get Al's boss's approval before being sent to the board of directors. Al worked to get the economic packages in the correct format for the board of directors. No one working for the company knew what Al and his boss did; no approval for spend went forward to the board of directors without Al's boss's approval. Al's boss was a genius with math. He had a master's degree in math and he just did the math before his approval. He ensured the company could make money and lots of money. Risk were not mitigated along the way, risk were planned for. Markets and product prices were defined before approval. Profits were the only reason to approve spending of any kind.

The company made Agent Orange that was used to defoliate the jungles in Viet Nam. This took away hiding places for the enemy. Agent Orange killed everything and had a long time effect in killing soldiers exposed to it. When Al learned the company made Agent Orange he cringed at the thought of working as part of a company that killed so quiet and secret but the full effects of AO would not be known for years when the old soldiers started dying from the same cancers and causes. Al started planning for a new job after finishing his college studies. The company told him he must also acquire a degree in chemical engineering. They had plans for him but now he must be educated in chemical engineering.

His first two years had required him to work all day and go to night classes at the university. The work and school was grinding and amounted to a 16 hour work day. Although he enjoyed it because it he could hide his transition from soldier to civilian. His plan wasn't working because he still slept with a gun under his pillow but felt a little better knowing he had transitioned from a large pistol to a small pistol that he still carried to work with him. The transitioning was not changing his reaction to threats and confrontations. The transition from soldier to civilian was neither fast nor easy. He took a second job so he could do his studies homework. On weekends he worked as a security guard for a bank. Locked up inside the bank he could study and complete homework. Inside a locked up bank was a place where he felt secure and could focus on studies. One night that secure feeling changed when someone knocked on the banks front door. Al opened the door and the man asks if he could use the bathroom. Al said yes and told him where the bathroom was. The man observed Al did not have a weapon and when he returned from the bathroom he stood in front of Al and said "gives me your wallet." Al reached in his pocket took out his small gun and told him. "I am going to put this in the middle of the desk, if you can get it before I do you can have my wallet, if you can't I will shoot you thru your heart." Al took out his small gun and placed it middle of the desk; the man looked at the gun, turned around and walked out of the bank. Al became so angry with his self and thought about taking some college courses in anger management. He couldn't find any night time classes for anger management but he did find classes in criminal ology and psychology. He registered for classes and discovered that most of his classmates were policemen trying to get a promotion but Al found the students and the subject studies to be very interesting.

It was during these studies Al learned who Carlos was. The professor had asked during the first class if anyone had any questions. Most of the cops ask about new laws and new penalties for breaking the laws. Al asked the professor "who killed President Kennedy?" The class laughed and the professor smiled. He ask Al why he ask the question and Al told his it was because it seemed that no one really knew who killed the President or why they killed him. The class and the Professor agreed with Al. The next week the Professor made assignments to all the students and he requested that Al prepare a report on the Joe Valachie book. Al read the book three times before he started his report.

Joe was a born and raised mafia. He wasn't wise or smart but he possessed one asset that saved his life. He had a photographic memory. He could remember people, events and places. When the mafia tried to kill him he turned rat and told the FBI about people, mafia chain of commands and unsolved mysteries than the FBI had not learned about in the previous 100 years. The FBI was given a map of the mafia and investigations started that put thousands of mafia in jail. The mob didn't die but they were severely

wounded. Joe spent the remainder of his life in jail.
The book fascinated Al and he paid special attention
to the names and their history.

The oldest mob in America was in New Orleans.
They started in 1857 and continue until today. Carlos
was the head of the New Orleans mob and the skinny
man he talked to on the airplane ride was the man
in charge of the Dallas mafia. Carlos was born in not
in Italy but Tunisia and came to America when he
was 3 years old. He grew up working in his father's
farm raising vegetables. Most of the vegetables were
sold to the U.S. Navy. When Robert Kennedy the
attorney General serving under his brother President
John Kennedy investigated the mafia because of East
Coast racketeering, all trails seemed to go thru New
Orleans and Carlos. It became clear that Carlos was
the Godfather of the entire American mafia. Robert
Kennedy arrested Carlos and had him deported to
Guatemala but he returned in a short period of time
and shortly thereafter President Kennedy was killed
in Dallas; all trails to who killed President Kennedy
ran thru New Orleans and Carlos but he was never
charged with anything and never again imprisoned or

deported from America. Al couldn't imagine Carlos killing President Kennedy but he couldn't imagine President Kennedy being killed without Carlos's approval.

The choice to take a couple of elective classes paid dividends in learning who really killed President Kennedy. President Kennedy was the only American President that Al could identify with and the day he was killed was one of the saddest days of his life. The day he met Carlos was one of the most life changing days of his life because he knew that he didn't have to become another homeless disabled veteran; all he had to do was go to New Orleans and see Carlos. Al knew that his service to America and his dreams for America were defined by President Kennedy and he also knew that he had been jointly responsible for killing more men than Carlos. It didn't matter who Carlos was because Carlos was the one man who stood up and offered him unconditional help when most of America turned its back on its soldiers. Al never doubted that President Kennedy would have done the same thing Carlos did if he had not been killed.

ROSES OF SHARON

Neil needed some supplies for the farm. His neighbor's cows had destroyed a part of the barbed wire fence and the neighbors cows had come into his pasture for free lunches. Free lunches are never free and the money spent planting good grass and the fertilizers to make it grow were expensive. The neighbor never spent any money improving his pasture and his cows never missed an opportunity to get a free lunch at Neil's expense. The irresponsibility of the neighbor was a constant source of bad feelings that ranged from shooting the neighbors cows to going to court to demand payment for the free lunches but it was Neil's choice to just turn the neighbors cows out to public land and to call the county animal control and report cows grazing along the busy highway. The farm was located a few miles from the county sheriff's office so the deputies usually responded quickly and notified the owner with a warning. Neil loved cows and his anger to his neighbor was because every winter his neighbor did not adequately feed his cows and some of the cows died from starvation. This was also reported to animal control but no action was ever taken by county officials unless the dead cows were not properly disposed. Usually the dead cows were eaten by the coyotes and buzzards. When Neil was driving into town for fence repair supplies his thoughts were how to get his neighbor imprisoned for animal abuse. The road into town ran by the county jail and near the jail he spotted a woman walking down the road. The county had a rule that anyone being released must have someone to pick them up. Sometimes the new released jail birds would lie about someone picking them up and just start walking the 5 miles into town. Sometimes Neil would stop and offer them a ride to town and sometimes he would give them a ride to their home. He enjoyed hearing their conversations about being in jail and the details of their arrest. Most had been arrested because of being drunk or using drugs. On one such occasion he knew the family of the jailed person, on another occasion he knew the jailed person, and on another occasion the jailed person was sent to jail after a report to police by Neil's own sister-in-law. Some had their shirts and shoes stolen while in jail and bare foot walking on any surface is difficult for city folks. Whenever Neil picked up a hitch hiker from the jail, it was always good honest conversation.

On the day he saw the short portly woman he stopped to offer her a ride into town because he thought she had just been released from jail but she said this was not the case. She said her car had run out of gas and she was going to her daughter's work place to get help. She said she needed to be at work by 4 pm; she worked at the local hospital in insurance claims; she had already walked 4 miles in the Texas heat and that she was pregnant. She also said that she had grown up in Chicago. Neil drove her to the place of her daughter's employer but upon arrival she said that her daughter was not there because her car was not in the parking lot. He told her that he would drive her back to her car and buy her some gas. As they drove she told him that her gas can was at her home and it was near the gas station. He drove her to her car and her home he thought of the town of Rosharon. The small town where she lived was named Rosharon but its original name was Roses of Sharon and the rail road people called it "Buttermilk station." It was founded before the civil war and somehow remained alive after the railroads died. It was an old train station town but the rail road had abandoned the tracks and the town had not had rails or service for years. At one time the trains running from Velasco to Harrisburg stopped in Rosharon and the east/west lines ran across the Brazos River and up to Richmond and down to Galveston but the trains had lost their value and the cotton plantations became cattle ranches. Highways and roads had replaced the railroads and the town nearly died. The old hotel remained but it was now a resale shop. The grain silos that were built by the railroad were still in use for storage of grain. The town had been mapped out with blocks and streets by an investor more than 100 years ago but over the years the streets made from oyster shells had decomposed and the only resemblance remaining were the perfect aligned streets and blocks. The streets had been named but their names had long been forgotten. The town was run down and all the original homes were gone and most of the habitat was in travel trailers or mobile homes but the trailers were so old none of them were travel worthy. The town had seen its better days and in a few more years Houston would swallow it like a whale swallowing small fish. Houston had already swallowed the place where General Sam Houston defeated the Mexican army commanded by the Mexican General Santa Anna. The birth place of Texas was just a few miles north east from Roses of Sharon. The site of the battle of San Jacinto where Texas earned its freedom was well chosen and the surrounding Bayou's ensured there would be no retreats on either side. The fight would be until death or unconditional surrender. The story tells of the "Yellow Rose" of Texas who helped Texas gain its independence. The real Yellow Rose was a mixed race beautiful woman who was known for her charm and beauty and the Mexican General Santa Anna was known for his sexual appetite both before and after a battle. General Santa Anna had lost one of his legs in battle and replaced it with a wooden leg but he was a first class soldier. A long story made short; The Yellow Rose of Texas was recruited by General Houston to service General Santa Anna and she made a hard man humble for hour after hour before the battle. The attack by General Houston caught Santa

Anna not only by surprise but with his pants down. The Yellow Rose would become a much loved state flower and the song "Yellow Rose of Texas" would be sung by every child growing up in Texas. The Roses of Sharon would be the most hated roses in Texas. One hundred years ago some lady living in Rosharon was in love with Roses. She surrounded her home with roses and over the years some of her roses went wild and started growing in the river bottoms, bayous, hay fields and cattle pastures. Her roses could survive and thrive in the Gulf Coast gumbo soil and hot, humid temperatures and the seldom hard frost and freezes didn't seem to impede their growth. The local people knew to not go near the Roses of Sharon; they burned them when possible. The roses were also known as Cherokee roses even though no Cherokee Indians had ever lived in Rosharon because the Native Americans who lived in the area were the only known cannibals in North America. It was no accident that the original Spanish land grant to European settlers was also home to the cannibal Karawanka Indians. The Indians really frightened the Spanish explorers and they avoided the area. Because the strong vines and sharp thorns the roses of Sharon they could rip into your skin and draw blood, the roses of Sharon were survivors.. The thorns could tear thru a pair of leather gloves. The pink roses of Sharon were hated as much as by the Texans as the Yellow Roses were loved.

Neil had been ripped by Sharon's roses and somehow he thought it was happening again. The lady in his truck from Rosharon story was not adding up. Neil turned and looked at her for the first time. She was a Yellow Rose from Chicago. Her story got more complicated. They continued talking as he looked her over. She was a beauty and when she told him that she was born and raised in Chicago but she never knew her parents until years later and her childhood had been spent in many foster homes. After she left foster care she located her father and mother and was told by them that they wanted nothing to do with her. Neil could not determine her race but her voice told him the story was true because she spoke with a Chicago south side accent. She noticed Neil observing her and she promptly looked into his eyes and said "I really need 20 dollars to pay my baby sitter, is there anything I can do for you to earn 20 dollars?" Neil looked into her blue eyes and quietly said "twenty years ago I can't imagine what you could not do but I am too old for

20 dollars of pleasure, so I respectfully turn down your proposal." She seem moved by his honesty but the moment was lost when he ask her how many children did she have. She said nine. She said her oldest son was in the Army, her oldest daughter didn't live at home but she had 7 children living at home. Their ages ran from 4 to 16 and she was pregnant. Her husband was from Rosharon but he had abandoned her and the kids. She told him this as they drove up the street to her home. As they got near the old trailer house kids of all ages and sizes were playing in the yard. The oldest told them all "Get in the house, mama is home and she told us to stay in the house." The scene reminded Neil of an old mother chicken trying to get all her baby chicks under her wings but he could see and feel the love and respect. She quickly got a 5 gallon gas can and they drove to the nearby gas station where Neil filled the can. Neil knew the Bombay Indian who ran the gas station because he usually stayed in the bullet proof cage inside the store and was reluctant to come out for any reason but today Neil didn't go inside. As they drove back to where her car ran out of gas, her story took another turn. The car wasn't a car at all, it was truck and it was parked at her neighbors place

with the back wheels missing. Neil unloaded the gas can and quickly got back in his truck and unbuckled his 45 cal pistol. Too many things didn't add up so he suspicioned foul play ahead. Maintaining his thoughts he reached into his pocket and handed the mysterious woman 50 dollars and told her "I hope to hell you ain't a drug head." No one setting on the neighbor's porch saw him hand her money. Somewhere along the road home, he realized what had happened. As strange as it seemed the woman did have 7 kids at home, she was pregnant, she was under 40 years old, she did grow up in Chicago and Neil was pretty sure that when he picked her up she had just been released from jail and she was every bit as dangerous as the Roses of Sharon but every bit as beautiful as the Yellow Rose of Texas.

POEMS THAT MAKE NO SENSE

Hedab 101

There was once a warm spot in my heart.

I can feel it slowly slipping away

Like a bed of burning charcoal.

It will be gone in a few more days.

I was amazed when it started to burn.

I had no idea what was inside me.

The flame grew to a tempered peak,

Enough to warm everyone beside me.

I guess we can call it life,

When all our fuel has burned out.

I know the flame once burned high

With a heat that no one could doubt.

When you see those white ashes

Blowing about in the wind,

Remember the fire they once held.

It burned in a place free of cold,

For everyone, including my friend Eyelashes.

Hedab 102

I felt so unloved and lonely.

Everyone I knew said goodbye.

I drifted around the world,

Looking for something new to try.

Then I met you almost by chance.

Our paths crossed like stars in the night.

We were so different, completely so:

You, a Muslim woman, wanting to grow;

Me, a cowboy with wild oats to sow.

For a while, time stood still,

Our days spent soaking up each other's soul.

I felt so warm and alive.

You gave me a spirit of want and truth.

Now it's over, like it never happened at all,

A sweet dream that could never come true.

Two years have passed, and I have forgotten,

But when I dream, I dream of you.

Hedab 103

Contentment is my most feared dragon; if I accept, I
will surely die.

I must fight until I can no longer stand; there is little
reason why.

I will retrace the trails of my youth, experience the
feel for what I lost,

Regain the fears of a cruel world, risk it all and damn
the cost.

The haunting fires inside my soul, they are but a spark
of heat I so need.

Go back to the past I knew to examine my wildest
seed.

The wax runs down the burning candle,

And it's almost cool before it stops.

So it is with life.

The birds work hard to build a nest, to hatch eggs of
its own.

As soon as the young can fly, they fly off into the sky.

To meet their needs of the day, winds carry them
separate ways.

No chance to say goodbye.

So it is with life.

ALAN NEIL

Hedab 104

I feel the energy start in my feet.
It moves up my body to my brain.
It intensifies before transmission,
Up to the sky and away.
I send as hard as I can,
Wanting it to reach you,
To cool your cheeks and wipe your tears
As cool, clean water can do.
I know the miles between us are many,
And many powers must be crossed,
But if I can send this through the air,
My soul will never be lost.
I don't know when this will get through,
But when you feel energy not your own,
Lift up your heart and smile.
It's a message from me.

Hedab 105

Palestine and its rolling brown hills
Have at last touched our hearts.
The history is discussed in length,
Its people are far apart.

The ocean cleans its beaches,
And its orange trees grow free,
But the hearts of its people
Can't let history be.

Home is where the heart is;
So simple yet so true.
For thousands of years, it hasn't changed.
All will die, but some will never know
The brown hills and green valleys of Palestine.

Hedab 106

The days pass so quickly,
And sometimes I am afraid
Of what tomorrow will bring
To this tired and lonely soul of mine.

The years have been good to me.
My children are proof that I see
My God has given me so much.
My God has made me free.

I am afraid to think of dying.
It's a trip we all must make,
But I know that sometimes it's harder
If we allow even one mistake.

Hedab 107

The old man cried and shook his head,
Said that life has passed him by.
I couldn't speak. I felt weak,
But I wanted to ask him why.

Twenty years later, I thought,
How fast can a life be?
I went to see family and friends
Buried in a cemetery:

People I have known and respected;
People of honor and truth;
People of all ages and faces,
Gone back to a box of bones.

As I looked at the graves,
I felt I was all alone,
Just waiting for someone
Who was already gone.

Hedab 108

I have no right to love you.
I know my feelings are astray,
But my heart knows no answer
To why I feel this way.

I could say *maybe* or *what if*
Or simply that it happened like this:
My heart belongs to a woman
I can never touch or kiss.

No one knows the future.
Even if our days are like the sand,
It could happen that we are together
If it's a part of God's plan.

Hedab 109

I miss you in so many ways
But none so great as others.
Your presence is always with me.
I feel the stare of your eyes.

I am not such a simple man
Because I am so much for so many.

My job is to give my children time
And fill their horn of plenty.

But sometimes when I am alone,
I think only of you.
I look to the sky and ask God why.
Your love goes through and through my soul.

Hedab 110

A little girl of two years old ran away in the dark of
    night.
Her family went to K8; she grew up in a stage of
    fright.
But as she grew, she grew so special, one of a kind I
    would say.
Her days had no security, and at night she seemed so
    far away
From her home in Palestine.

When I came to know her, I said, "Oh, little girl, I
    want to help you,
But I am a tumbleweed in the wind. My home is the
    prairie,
And the sky is my only friend.

I have always been so proud of myself, until I found
a love like you,
And there is nothing I won't do for you, or nothing
I can do
Except love you."

Hedab 112

The country was lost forever, at least it seemed.
Many had fought and died to avoid the horrible dream.
Still it happened, and no one could tell why.
The home of my friend Eyelashes was allowed to die.

Then something magical happened that bombs
couldn't do.
A brand-new country came into view, first in the
minds of many,
Then into the land of plenty.

The prayers of women and children changed
everything.
It wasn't world powers but world hearts that needed
to be won.

Printed in the United States
By Bookmasters